The troub

Frances couldn't
talking back to Alb
was beginning to fe
at her and said, "Where're your specs?"

"Specs?" Frances squeaked.

"Yeah, you know, glasses."

All Frances's newfound confidence began oozing out of her.

"In my backpack."

"When are we going to get a look-see?"

You? Frances thought. Never.

"Frances Four-Eyes," Albert began singing, "loves all the boys…"

Frances four-eyes

by
ILENE COOPER
Illustrated by Vilma Ortiz

BULLSEYE BOOKS • ALFRED A. KNOPF

NEW YORK

A BULLSEYE BOOK PUBLISHED BY ALFRED A. KNOPF, INC.

Library of Congress Cataloging-in-Publication Data
Cooper, Ilene.
Frances Four-eyes / by Ilene Cooper.
p. cm.—(Frances in the fourth grade)
Summary: A shy fourth grader becomes more assertive as she dances
the lead role at a recital, suggests a community project in class,
and starts to wear her new glasses.
ISBN: 0-679-81112-5 (pbk.) — ISBN 0-679-91112-X (lib. bdg.)
[1. Eyeglasses—Fiction. 2. Bashfulness—Fiction. 3. Schools—
Fiction.] I. Title. II. Title: Frances Four-eyes. III. Series:
Cooper, Ilene. Frances in the fourth grade.
PZ7.C7836Fp   1991   [Fic]—dc20   90-28270
RL: 4.4
First Bullseye Books edition: November 1991

Manufactured in the United States of America
10 9 8 7 6 5 4 3 2 1

Frances four-eyes

1

Snow, snow, and more snow. Frances McAllister looked out the window and watched a new batch of flakes float down lazily and settle on the mounds of white already on the ground.

It wasn't that Frances wasn't used to snow. If you lived in Wisconsin your whole life, you knew that winter meant snow. But it had been snowing every day for more than a week, and Frances was ready for it to stop—at least for a little while.

"So what do you think, Frances?" Mr. Winnow's voice invaded Frances's frost-filled thoughts.

She turned toward her teacher, wishing she had the faintest idea what he was asking her about. Her eyes darted over to her friend, Polly Brock, who was pointing frantically to her stomach.

"I—I don't know what I'm having for lunch," Frances replied in desperation.

The class burst out laughing.

Mr. Winnow frowned. "I'm not concerned about your lunch, Frances. What we were discussing—before you left us," he added pointedly, "was our plans for the community outreach program."

Frances wrinkled her nose. Someone at Lake Lister Elementary School, probably Mrs. Rotterdam, the civic-minded principal, had decided that each grade should pitch in and come up with a project to help the community. Frances's sister, Elizabeth, was in the sixth grade and they had decided to shovel snow for the elderly residents of Lake Lister. Well, they couldn't have picked a better winter for it.

"Tammi suggested we help out at the soup kitchen." *Now* Frances understood Polly's frantic gesture. "How do you feel about that?" Mr. Winnow asked. This was his first year of teaching, but he was getting good at figuring out how to put kids on the spot when necessary.

"That would be good," Frances said.

"Do you have any other ideas?"

Frances shook her head. She had forgotten that Mr. Winnow had made an idea for the outreach project today's assignment. Quickly she tried to think of some wonderful, helpful activity, but Mr. Winnow had already turned away. He called on Albert Bell, who was wildly waving his hand.

As far as Frances was concerned, Albert Bell, the class tease, was nothing but a big pain. When he wasn't making fun of her for being short, he was tangling with Polly. But unlike shy Frances, Polly could give Albert back some of his own and more.

Albert jumped to his feet, his freckles practically quivering on his face. "I think we should raise money for an aquarium."

"That wouldn't be because you'd like to have a shark here in Lake Lister, would it, Albert?" Mr. Winnow asked with a sigh.

Frances knew the answer to that question. Albert was shark crazy. Books on sharks were the only kind he ever checked out of the library, and he was always hunched over his desk drawing pictures of the dangerous fish. Lately the sharks were swimming menacingly behind girls who looked suspiciously like Polly and Frances.

"Lake Lister could use a shark," Albert argued.

"I believe you're possibly the only resident who thinks so," Mr. Winnow said. "Besides, towns of our size usually don't have aquariums."

"This town doesn't have anything," Albert muttered as he sat down.

As usual, Frances didn't agree with Albert. She liked Lake Lister. In the summer it was a tourist town. People from Milwaukee and even as far away as Chicago came to enjoy the lake and the quaint shops. But in the winter Lake Lister returned to the residents. Maybe there were no museums or aquariums, but you could skate on the lake, go sledding, or see a movie out at the mall. Frances didn't see what else anyone would want to do.

Mr. Winnow paced in front of his desk. "Frankly, class, I'm a little disappointed in your suggestions for a community project."

Frances lowered her eyes so Mr. Winnow wouldn't single her out. But his eyes scanned the room, including everyone.

"Mrs. Rotterdam wants our decision by the beginning of next week, and I think we can do better. We can certainly come up with more suggestions at any rate. So I want all of you to put on your thinking caps and we'll discuss this further tomorrow."

Albert Bell mimed putting on a hat that was so heavy his head rolled around on his neck. Mr. Winnow ignored him.

"Boy, that Albert Bell is getting more and more obnoxious," Polly said later at the lunch table. She took a big bite out of her ham and cheese sandwich.

"An aquarium." Frances sniffed. "Maybe we should get a zoo so we could put Albert in it."

Lena Kroll looked around nervously. "He might hear you." Lena had only been in Lake Lister—in America, actually—for about a year. She had come from an Eastern European country, and she still had a slight accent.

"Oh, who cares!" Polly tossed her dark curls. "What can he do to us?"

Over the years Albert had done plenty to Frances. He called her McShrimp, he had pulled her braids before she got her hair cut, and most recently he had been a pain at ballet school.

Except for the presence of Albert, Frances loved taking lessons at Miss Leticia's School of the Dance. Albert was Miss Leticia's nephew, and she had made him join because she needed some boys in the class. He had quit ballet before Christmas, though, which was making lessons a lot more fun.

"I think Lena's right," Frances said. "We should just stay out of Albert's way."

Polly shook her head in disdain. "*I* don't stay out of anybody's way. Let Albert stay out of *my* way."

Even though Frances couldn't share Polly's attitude, it was one of the things she admired about her. The very first time Albert had started in with Polly, she had made up—and recited—a little poem in which "Bell" rhymed with "smell."

When Polly had first arrived in Lake Lister at the end of the summer, Frances never thought the two of them would become friends. They were opposites in just about everything. Polly was big and brash, while Frances was small and shy. Polly liked being center stage, whereas Frances felt more comfortable in the background. But oddly, the closer they became, the more each seemed to take on the other's characteristics. Frances wasn't quite as timid as she once was, and though Polly was still a tease, she was much more careful about hurting people's feelings. That didn't mean, however, that she wouldn't stand up to Albert Bell.

"Well, I'm just glad Albert stopped coming to ballet lessons," Frances said fervently.

"How many boys do you have now?" Lena asked curiously.

"None. There used to be a boy named Simon, but he broke his arm."

"Are you still going to have a recital?" Lena asked. She was too nice to be jealous, but she did look a little wistful.

"Yes," Frances said happily. "We're going to do a dance where a boy and a girl go into the forest and meet the animals."

"We spent practically one whole lesson hopping around like rabbits," Polly remembered, shaking her head.

"And Albert kept hopping into you."

"Yeah. A real funny bunny."

"My parents are going to let me start taking lessons in the spring." Lena's parents were strict and liked her to spend most of her time on schoolwork. But Frances knew she had been begging to be allowed to take ballet. She was glad the Krolls had finally given their permission.

"It will be great," Frances promised.

"You could start lessons again, Polly," Lena suggested.

"Not me. You never saw me in a leotard."

Polly *was* a little too large to look good in a ballet outfit, but Frances still wished Polly would reconsider. Everything was more fun when Polly was doing it too. But Polly had hated ballet so much, Frances knew there wasn't any chance of her rejoining the class.

"It would be great if you came," Frances said, "but as long as Albert stays away, I'll be happy."

"No dancing. But why don't we go ice-skating after school?" Polly suggested. "It's perfect weather for it."

"Great." Frances was getting pretty good at skating. "Can you go, Lena?"

"I think so," Lena said. "We don't have much homework, and my parents think ice-skating is good exercise."

So after school the girls stopped at their houses, picked up their skates, and headed over to the part of the lake that was set up for ice-skating.

Frances had just finished lacing her skates when she looked up and noticed Albert Bell and Steve

Sanders whizzing by. Steve was in one of the other fourth-grade classes, but Frances knew that he was almost as big a tease as Albert.

Frances nudged Lena. "Let's stay away from them," she whispered as she gestured in the boys' direction.

Lena nodded. "Fine with me."

Polly overheard the conversation. "Don't be silly. If they bother us, we'll bother them right back." Determinedly, she got up and skated toward the middle of the ice. Frances and Lena followed.

For a while the girls just skated around making lazy circles on the ice. Then they started a game of tag. They had only been playing a few moments when Albert slid over to them and poked Frances hard on the shoulder. "You're it."

Frances tried to glide away from him, but she wasn't nearly as good a skater as Albert. "You're it," he said, poking her again. Then it was Steve's turn to poke her. "You're it, Frances." He laughed, then turned and skated over to Lena, banging against her. "You're it, too."

Polly had been circling around the edge of the lake, but now she plowed forward. "Hey, go play your own game."

Polly's hat fell off, and Albert picked it up. Then he tossed it to Steve, who tossed it right back to Albert over Polly's head.

"Come on, girls, let's get him." Polly motioned to Frances and Lena.

For a few seconds they just stood there, but then they skated over to Polly. "You go that way," she directed Frances. "Lena, try to cut Albert off."

Frances expected to be scared, but instead she felt a surge of excitement. Heading where Polly motioned, she found herself behind Albert. Lena was in front of him, keeping Steve from getting close. Then Polly skated up and covered Albert, also blocking Steve. Seeing he was surrounded, Albert tried to dart between the girls, but they closed ranks, forcing him to skate backward. Albert was a pretty good skater, but not that good. He fell down with a thump.

"Ow!" he cried, rubbing his backside.

While he was distracted, Polly whisked her hat out of his pocket. Frances and Lena cheered. Then they skated to the bank. Frances looked over her shoulder to see if the boys were following her, but Steve and Albert were near the rope guards, ignoring them.

"That'll show Albert Bell who he can mess with," Polly said with satisfaction.

"You don't think he's hurt, do you?" soft-hearted Lena asked.

"No." Polly's tone was scornful. "He's got a hide like an elephant. Besides, he started it."

The girls skated a while longer, keeping an eye out for another ambush, but it appeared that the boys had left. Soon, however, it was too dark to see where they were going. Lately Frances had a little trouble seeing anyway. The horrible thought had struck her that maybe she needed glasses, but she wasn't going to mention it to anyone.

By the time Frances got home, dinner was almost ready. Elizabeth was putting the salad on the table, and their mother was taking the tuna-noodle casserole out of the oven. The cord from the kitchen phone stretched through the doorway into the dining room. That meant Mike was on the phone, where he had been a lot lately. Frances suspected he had a girlfriend. Usually when he had telephone conversations with his friends, he was so loud you could hear him a couple of houses down. But Frances noticed recently that he spoke in hushed whispers.

"Guess what?" Frances said, pulling off her coat and hanging it on the hook next to the back door.

"You forgot to get home in time to set the table?" Elizabeth asked sourly.

"I'll clear after dinner," Frances said.

"You heard that, Mom," Elizabeth crowed. "Frances is clearing the table."

Mrs. McAllister looked harried. "Yes, somebody has to. I have to go down to the store after dinner and help your father take inventory. Mike does too."

McAllister's Hardware was on Main Street. Many of the stores closed down after the tourist season, but the hardware store stayed open all year selling ladders and nails and shovels. It used to be a busy, bustling place, but since the mall had been built outside of town, many people went to the big hardware store there. For what seemed like a very long time, Mr. McAllister had been complaining about business falling off. Frances didn't like to see her dad so glum. He was usually such a jolly father, always ready to play a game of checkers with her or take her swimming or sledding.

"I think I'll wash up," Frances said.

"Yes, do that," her mother replied. "Your father will be home any minute."

Frances passed by Mike, who was sprawled out on the dining room floor, the phone hugging his ear. She could hear him, but just barely.

"I'll pick you up about eight," he whispered.

Frances stopped and listened with interest.

"A movie, I guess." Then he noticed Frances trying to look inconspicuous.

He put his hand over the phone. "Scat."

"I'm not doing anything."

"You're listening. Beat it."

Frances moved on, shaking her head. Since Mike had started high school in the fall, he had sure changed. Suddenly he was always looking in the mirror and asking Mrs. McAllister if he could buy a new shirt or sweater. And now this whispering on the phone. Frances hoped that when she got into high school she wouldn't turn weird.

By the time she got back downstairs, everyone was seated at the table. Mike was already digging into the tuna-noodle casserole, but he didn't seem very happy about it.

"When are we going to have something good?" he grumbled.

"What's wrong with my casserole?" Mrs. Mc-Allister asked.

"It's not steak."

"Steak's expensive," Mr. McAllister said. "The way business is going, we're lucky we've got this."

Elizabeth rolled her eyes. "Oh, Dad, let's not talk about the store again, please."

Her father gave her a half smile. "Believe me, I

hate talking about how bad business is just as much as you hate hearing about it."

Frances tried to think of something to change the subject. "Mike's got a date."

This was the wrong topic. Mike glared at her. "Hey, what do you know about it, bigmouth?"

"Mike's got a girlfriend," Elizabeth sang.

"Mom . . ." Mike complained.

"Your brother is right," Mrs. McAllister said, her tone stern. "I don't want you teasing him about his social life." But she had a small smile on her face when she said it.

"I was about your age, Mike, when I started dating your mother." Mr. McAllister reached over and patted his wife's hand.

The kids exchanged glances. They could never believe how mushy their parents still were.

Mr. McAllister picked up his fork and dug into his salad. "But maybe you should have married Joe Porter. He's a dentist in Milwaukee now. You could have been living on easy street."

"Gee, I don't recall any Easy Street in Milwaukee," Mrs. McAllister joked.

"At least you wouldn't be worrying about how many nuts and bolts I sold," he said, looking glum.

"No, I'd be worrying about people not having enough cavities," his wife answered pertly.

Seeing her mother trying so hard to cheer up her dad—and her dad looking so discouraged—gave Frances a strange, unsettled feeling in her stomach. It was as if the tuna-noodle casserole had decided to sit there permanently. Mr. McAllister might not say any more this evening about business falling off, but Frances knew that the family hadn't heard the end of the topic.

2

❝ Oh, don't worry about your dad's business,"
Polly said. "My dad complains about business all the
time." The girls were on the school bus. Frances had
been filling Polly in on the problems of the hardware
store.

Polly's parents were divorced, and her father lived
in Milwaukee. Frances wasn't sure what he did, but
he seemed to own several companies. "One of your
dad's businesses could go bad, and he'd still have a
couple of others. All my father has is the hardware
store."

"Maybe we could think of ways to get people to
buy stuff."

"Like what?"

"I don't know. Throw things down their plumb-
ing?" Polly joked.

Frances allowed herself a smile. "We could pull
the nails out of people's houses. Hey, maybe that
could be our class's community project." The girls
laughed.

"Have you thought of a project?" Frances asked.

"Yes. Well, actually my mother came up with something. Collect books for the library book sale." Polly's mother was the head librarian at the Lake Lister library.

"That's good. I thought we could collect clothes for the people that needed them."

Later that day Frances was glad that she had thought of at least one idea. Mr. Winnow went around the room asking everyone to give their suggestions. He wrote them all on the blackboard.

"Let's think about these. Maybe we can come up with a few more."

As she sat at the back of the room, Frances noticed that once again Mr. Winnow's writing looked fuzzy. She wished he'd write with a steadier hand. It was so hard to figure out what was on the board. Math was the next period, and Mr. Winnow used what was left of the blackboard to explain how to divide fractions. She tried to copy down his examples, but she didn't know if he had written one fourth or one ninth. Timidly she raised her hand and asked which he meant.

Mr. Winnow looked concerned. "Can't you see the board, Frances?"

"Sure I can see it," she said with embarrassment.

He motioned her forward. "Come up here. Does it look clearer now?"

Frances moved to the front of the class, feeling everyone's eyes on her back. "Oh, it's one fourth."

"Maybe you need to have your eyes checked, Frances. I'll write your mother a note suggesting it."

Frances groaned to herself. How could she have been so silly as to call attention to her vision problems? When Mr. Winnow gave her the note to take home, she stuffed it in her knapsack and promptly forgot about it.

Tuesdays always went by slowly for Frances. She had ballet lessons after school and she could hardly wait to get there. When the bell finally rang, she waved good-bye to Polly and Lena and hurried off to Miss Leticia's.

Frances practically had to pass right by her father's hardware store to get to Miss Leticia's, and she usually stuck her head inside just to say hello. Today she hoped her father might be too busy with customers to talk, but there he was, just standing behind the counter, leafing through a catalog.

"Hi, Daddy," Frances said, coming into the store.

Her father smiled at her. "I thought you might be a customer. But I'd rather see you any day of the week."

She went over to him and gave him a kiss. "How's business today?"

Mr. McAllister made a face. "I think everybody must be out of town. You off to ballet?"

She dangled the bag with her shoes, tights, and leotard in front of him. "Where else?"

"When's this big recital I keep hearing about?"

"Next month. Miss Leticia is going to announce the parts today," Frances informed him happily.

"Hope you get a good one."

Secretly Frances had her heart set on being the lead, the little girl who wanders through the forest.

But Tammi Elliot would probably get it. Tammi was the kind of girl who always got everything she wanted.

"I better go. I don't want to be late."

But when Frances walked into Miss Leticia's, a terrible sight met her eyes. Standing at the barre, wearing sweatpants and a *Jaws* T-shirt, was none other than Albert Bell.

She was dying to ask him what he was doing there, but she was afraid of the answer. She tried hurrying past him, but Albert stuck out his foot, pretending to try and trip her.

"Hey, short stuff, aren't you glad to see me back?"

"No," Frances answered curtly.

Albert put a hurt expression on his face. "McShrimp, I thought you'd be happy."

"I thought you quit ballet," Frances finally said.

"Aw, my mother and aunt got together and made me start up again."

Last time Albert had been in the class it was because his aunt had bribed him with the promise of a bicycle. "What are you getting this time?" Frances asked.

"An aquarium," he said happily.

Frances shook her head and walked into the changing room. "Did you see who's here?" she asked.

Tammi was busy looking at herself in the mirror. She was always looking at herself. Polly said Tammi must love the studio because there were mirrors on every wall. "No, who?"

"Albert."

Tammi's best friend, Sheila, walked over. "Albert's back?"

"Yep. He's out there now. Waiting to pounce."

"Well," Tammi said, putting her long hair up in a bun, "I guess that means he's going to be in the recital. He'll either play the boy or the hunter."

Of course. Why hadn't she thought of that. Miss Leticia probably wanted a real boy to play the lead in their dance. He might play the hunter, she supposed, but Miss Leticia was certainly too smart to give Albert a role where he had a bow and arrow in his hand the whole time he was onstage. Disgustedly, Frances changed into her leotard. Now the recital was going to be ruined. She didn't even *want* to play the girl if it meant dancing with Albert. Not that you could call what he did dancing. Jumping around was more like it.

The girls began filtering out into the studio. Miss Leticia was already standing by the piano with the accompanist, Mrs. Morton. They couldn't have made an odder-looking pair. Miss Leticia was a striking woman with dramatic black hair. She always wore pretty outfits. Today it was a bright blue leotard and a long filmy skirt. Mrs. Morton was short and stocky and her dresses were usually some dark color, like gray or black. When she played their music, she banged away at the keys.

"All right, class," Miss Leticia said, turning toward them. "Let's begin our warmup exercises, *s'il vous plaît.*" Miss Leticia liked to throw in French phrases when she talked. By now Frances knew that "seel voo play" meant "please."

Frances looked warily over her shoulder. The class stood at the barre in order of height, and Albert was toward the back, while she was at the front. Nevertheless, she wanted to keep her eye on him.

The class moved through their exercises and practiced several steps. Miss Leticia walked up and down the line, giving suggestions and making corrections. When she got to Albert, Frances heard Miss Leticia say with a sigh, "Try to be a little more graceful, Albert."

Albert just snickered.

Frances always tried to be graceful. She concentrated on moving her arms and doing her steps as precisely and as well as possible. When she first started taking ballet lessons, it seemed as if she were about to step on her own feet, but she had practiced—at home and in class—and now the movements came more naturally to her. There were times (not always, but sometimes) when the movements and the music came together and Frances felt as if she were really dancing. That was wonderful.

When the class was nearly over, Miss Leticia clapped her hands. "You are improving! Now I am ready to announce who will play each role in our recital."

First she called off the names of the rabbits, then the foxes and birds. When Tammi's name was called as the hunter, Frances watched her frown. Tammi wanted to play the girl, not run around the stage with a bow and arrow, Frances guessed. She kept waiting for her own name to be called, but soon all the roles were cast except the two leads. Frances closed her eyes. Oh, no! she thought.

"The little girl will be played by Frances, and her brother, of course, by Albert."

Albert pretended to cough but was really saying "Shrimp, shrimp." Either Miss Leticia didn't get it or was just ignoring her nephew.

"I am planning the recital for around Valentine's Day, and that's a little more than a month away, so we must practice, practice, practice, *oui*? Frances and Albert, come over here." She motioned them forward.

Frances moved closer to Miss Leticia. Albert skipped up behind her.

"You don't have to skip yet, Albert," Miss Leticia said.

"But we do skip, right?" Albert asked innocently. "I was just practicing."

"Practice when I tell you to practice." For the first time Frances heard an edge to Miss Leticia's voice.

Albert turned so his aunt couldn't see him, and without even using his hands, turned his lips inside out and crossed his eyes at the class. There was some nervous laughter.

Miss Leticia could see that the class's attention was slipping away from her. "Let's begin. Rabbits, over here. Foxes behind them."

In their dance a brother and sister wander through the woods and become lost. They share their basket of food with several rabbits, foxes, and an owl. A hunter tries to hurt some of the animals, but the brother and sister save the beasts, who in turn help them out of the woods. Maybe Tammi didn't like her part, but Frances thought she might be good at it. Tammi could be pretty nasty when she wanted to be.

"Now, Albert and Frances, join hands. I want you to walk through the forest."

"I thought this is where we skip," Albert objected.

"I've reconsidered. I just want you to walk through the forest. Glide through, like this." Miss Leticia demonstrated what she wanted. It looked as if she were ice-skating on the wooden floor. She motioned to Mrs. Morton to begin playing.

If Miss Leticia thought that by removing skipping she was going to keep Albert from hamming it up, she was sadly mistaken. Grabbing Frances's arm, he glided all right, making long dramatic movements, one after another.

"I can't keep up with you," Frances whispered angrily.

"Your legs are too short," he whispered back.

"Make your glides closer together, Albert," Miss Leticia said, trying to clap time with the music.

Immediately Albert turned his glides into short, mincing little steps.

"No, longer than that." Miss Leticia walked over to Albert and spoke softly so that just Albert and Frances could hear her. "Glide, Albert, like a fish. Like a fish that swims in an aquarium."

Albert got the message. His glides assumed the proper proportions. That didn't stop him from making comments to Frances as they moved through the imaginary forest, pretending to pick flowers and smell them.

"I do smell something," Albert said, almost to himself.

Frances ignored him.

"I smell someone who has body odor." To anyone

else it looked as if Albert was sniffing a flower, but Frances knew that he was leaning over and smelling her.

"I don't smell!"

"No?" Albert lifted an eyebrow.

Frances could hardly wait until the lesson was over. As soon as Miss Leticia dismissed them, she hurried into the small bathroom off the dressing room and lifted her armpits. They smelled okay to her.

Glumly Frances went into the changing room and put on her clothes. All the way home she wondered how such a thing could have happened. She had wished and wished for the lead role in the recital, and now that she had it, it was ruined.

"Hey, did you get your part?" Elizabeth asked as soon as Frances walked through the door. Elizabeth was taking tap lessons, and her class was going to be in the recital too.

Frances told her what happened.

"Boy, I'm glad I don't have any boys in my class."

Mrs. McAllister, who was making a meat loaf, said, "Just tell that Albert not to act up or you'll report him to his aunt."

Frances looked at her mother pityingly. "If I do that, he'll just bug me even more."

"Maybe he teases you because he likes you," her mother suggested.

Frances didn't even dignify this suggestion with an answer. Instead she asked, "Can't we have hamburgers instead of meat loaf?"

"Meat loaf stretches," her mother answered shortly.

Privately Frances thought the reason meat loaf

stretched into leftovers was because nobody liked it. But she knew her mother tried very hard to make meals on a small budget, so she didn't say anything else.

"Why don't you girls get started on your homework?" It was more an order than a suggestion.

Frances and Elizabeth grabbed their book bags and headed upstairs. On the way past their parents' bedroom they saw Mike talking on the phone. Mr. and Mrs. McAllister didn't like the kids to use the extension in their room, but sometimes for special calls they got permission. Frances wondered if Mike had secured permission or if he was sneaking a call.

"Do you know who his girlfriend is?" Frances whispered as they walked past.

Elizabeth shook her head. "It would be interesting to find out, though, wouldn't it?"

"I can't believe anyone would like Mike."

The girls looked at each other and giggled.

"If she could only see him running around in those torn flannel pajamas of his, with his hair all sticking up in the morning."

"Some boyfriend." Elizabeth laughed.

Before starting her homework, Frances changed into jeans and a sweatshirt and neatly hung up her school clothes. Elizabeth, on the other hand, flung what she was wearing onto the floor, atop a mountain of other soiled garments. A white cat darted out from under the mound.

"Snowflake!" Frances scooped up her kitten. "You almost buried her alive," she accused her sister.

"Well, she shouldn't have been under there in the first place."

"The *clothes* shouldn't have been there." Elizabeth's sloppiness was a real sore point.

"I'm creative," Elizabeth said haughtily. "Creative minds can't be bothered with straightening up."

"I'll tell Mom you said that." Frances pulled her books from her book bag and placed them neatly on her desk.

"Hey, you dropped something just now," Elizabeth said, picking up Mr. Winnow's note from the floor.

"Give it back."

"Why, what's in it?" Elizabeth asked curiously.

Frances didn't want her sister reading the note. She'd be all too likely to let slip Mr. Winnow's suggestion for an eye test. "None of your business," Frances said, grabbing for it.

But Elizabeth had already opened it up. " 'Frances is having trouble reading the board. I suggest you have her eyes tested.' Oh, big deal," Elizabeth said, flinging the note back at Frances.

But the damage had already been done. Mrs. McAllister stood in the doorway of the bedroom. "Why, Frances," she said. "We'd better make an appointment with the eye doctor."

3

frances looked out the car window. She was on her way to the eye doctor, and she wasn't at all happy about it.

When her mother had come in at that awful moment, Frances knew that there wasn't any way out of an appointment. She hadn't even tried to argue. Oh, maybe she had. Just a little.

"Mom, my eyes are fine," she had told her mother.

"Then why did Mr. Winnow write the note?" Mrs. McAllister asked.

"He's just being a teacher. I can't read his writing because it's so fuzzy."

"Mr. Winnow has very nice handwriting," Elizabeth interjected. "Look at the note."

Elizabeth had a crush on Mr. Winnow. So of course she liked everything about him. She even liked the way he dressed, despite the fact that he wore the same thing almost every day—plain white shirt, tan pants, corduroy jacket, and a wild tie.

But Mrs. McAllister wasn't interested in Elizabeth's

opinions on Mr. Winnow's handwriting. "Frances, what do you mean his writing is fuzzy?"

Frances knew then that she was in big trouble. "Oh," she mumbled, "it's just a little light and kind of, you know, fuzzy."

"I'll call Dr. Bemish tomorrow," Mrs. McAllister said. "Now come downstairs. It's time to eat."

"Mom," Frances whined. "I don't want to go to the eye doctor."

"I don't want to hear it, Frances. We're not going to play around with your eyesight."

So now Frances was wasting a perfectly good Saturday afternoon on her way to Dr. Bemish's office. The only good thing about it was that Polly was going along with her.

At the moment, though, Polly was leaning over the front seat and chatting with Mrs. McAllister, obviously unaware of the butterflies flitting around in Frances's stomach.

Frances clasped her hands together. What if she had to wear glasses? Last year Sandy Schuster, a girl in Frances's class, had shown up in glasses, and she looked totally dopey. She had gotten clear frames with what looked like pieces of glitter stuck inside them. Tammi had laughed at Sandy and said her grandmother wore the same kind of glasses. Albert had heard that and started calling Sandy Grandma. That's all Frances needed—one more excuse for Albert to tease her.

Frances turned around. "Hey, I need to talk to you about something."

"What?" Polly asked.

Frances whispered so her mother couldn't hear her.

"Do you think people will make fun of me if I wear glasses?"

Polly thought about it for a moment. "You mean call you four-eyes and stuff?"

Four-eyes. Frances Four-Eyes. She hadn't even thought of that gruesome possibility. "Yeah," Frances said with a sigh. "That's what I mean."

"Probably."

"Oh, Polly." Frances groaned.

"What are you two being so secretive about?" Mrs. McAllister asked.

"I'm not wearing glasses!" Frances cried. "People are going to tease me."

"Nobody will say anything."

Frances and Polly exchanged glances. That's how much mothers knew about the way things worked.

Mrs. McAllister caught their looks. "All right," she conceded. "Kids might tease a little. But it will all pass. And think how much easier your schoolwork will be if you can see the board properly."

Frances didn't care about seeing the board or any-thing else, for that matter. The only important thing was that kids didn't see her wearing glasses.

Polly leaned forward, her voice confidential. "We've got some real bigmouths in our class, Mrs. McAllister."

"I'm sure you do. But I think Frances can handle them. Certainly she can with your help, Polly."

Polly tried to look humble. "Well, nobody messes with me, that's for sure."

"Polly can't be with me every second," Frances said, kicking the door with her foot.

"Stop that," Mrs. McAllister scolded. "You can stick

up for yourself. Besides, your glasses will be very attractive. We'll make sure of it."

Frances closed her eyes. She imagined herself in glasses, all different kinds: skinny granny glasses, big heavy frames, wire aviator styles. It wasn't a pretty thought.

Dr. Bemish's office was in the medical building next to the hospital. Frances and Polly got dropped off while Mrs. McAllister parked the car. Polly led the way and Frances followed behind her, feeling as if she were on her way to her own execution.

"Boy, we're entering the Twilight Zone," Polly whispered, checking out the walls.

The waiting room looked like any other doctor's office except for one thing. There were pictures of eyes everywhere you turned. Black-and-white photos of single unblinking eyes and color closeups of eyes that were all different shades. One of the eyes was even pink. If that wasn't bad enough, the eyes followed you right around the room.

"It's a good thing this guy isn't a foot doctor," Polly said with a laugh as they took a seat.

Frances managed a weak smile. It was kind of funny, but Frances wasn't in a laughing mood.

Mrs. McAllister finally arrived, a little out of breath, gave Frances's name to the receptionist, and sat down next to them. "They'll call you in a few minutes. They're running just a little late," she said.

Which was worse? Frances wondered. Just getting the stupid test over with, or enjoying her last few moments as a glasses-less person?

"Want to play tick-tack-toe?" Polly asked, pulling a piece of paper and a pencil out of her backpack.

"I guess."

Frances didn't have her mind on the game. By the time her name was called by a perky nurse, Frances was losing four games to one.

Polly carefully folded up the piece of paper and stuck it in her backpack. She was like that. She kept everything. "Maybe the glasses will help you see the x's and o's better."

Maybe, but Frances doubted it.

"Do you want me to come in with you?" Mrs. McAllister asked.

Frances shook her head.

Her mother was pretty good about not treating her like a baby. She just nodded and picked up one of the magazines. "I'll come in after the exam."

A little nervously, Frances entered the examination room. There were no photos of eyes, but there was a big chair in the middle of the room that looked like a dentist's chair. Dr. Bemish was standing next to it. He was a small, balding man with an extremely cheerful look on his face.

"So, Frances, good to see you. And I hope you can see me."

Inwardly, Frances groaned. An eye doctor who thought he was a comedian.

"That's how I always say hello to my new patients. Have a seat."

Frances climbed into the chair. She was relieved to see there were no gleaming sharp silver instruments like there were at the dentist's office.

The first thing the doctor did was shut off the lights in the room and look at her eyes while holding what seemed to be a little flashlight. "Tell me, Frances, what do you have trouble seeing?" he asked as he examined her.

"The board," she mumbled.

"How about when you're walking down the street? Difficult to make things out sometimes?"

"Sometimes." She wasn't going to give Dr. Bemish any more ammunition than necessary.

"What about when you read a book?"

"That's okay."

"Fine," he said. "Now I'm going to give you a little test. It's very easy, Frances. I'll show you some letters on a chart, and you tell me if you can read them."

Dr. Bemish pulled down a chart that was on the far side of the room. Frances could read the first letter, a large *E*. But the letters in the next line were a little more difficult to make out.

"Uh, *F?*" Frances guessed. "*C, L, P?*" The letters were very fuzzy, just like Mr. Winnow's writing on the board.

After she had stumbled through a few more lines, Dr. Bemish pulled over a metal apparatus with two holes cut out and put it over her eyes. Then he slid lenses down over the holes for her to look through.

Frances was amazed. Why, the letters on the chart were completely different from the ones she had thought they were. Now she could see them and quickly rattled them off.

"Very good," Dr. Bemish said. "Now tell me if this makes things better or worse." For a few minutes he continued to switch lenses back and forth until her vision was very crisp and clear.

"I read the whole chart," she said wonderingly.

The doctor laughed. "Yes, that's what glasses do for you."

"Oh." Frances had been so excited by her ability to focus on the chart, she had forgotten that if she wanted to keep seeing like this, she would have to have glasses made.

"What's wrong?" Dr. Bemish asked as he wrote something down on a notepad.

"I—I don't want to wear glasses."

Dr. Bemish looked up with surprise. "But Frances, you can't do anything if your vision's impaired."

Frances didn't even bother to argue. What else would an eye doctor say? Of course he wanted her to wear glasses. He must have taken her silence for agreement because he patted her on the shoulder and called her mother into the examining room.

"Frances is nearsighted. I've written down a prescription for her," Dr. Bemish said, handing the piece of paper to Mrs. McAllister. "This should fix her up just fine. Wear your new glasses as much as possible, Frances, except when you're reading up close."

After thanking the doctor, Frances let herself be led into the waiting room. When she saw Polly, she shook her head.

Mrs. McAllister checked her watch. "We still have a little time before dinner. Shall we just go over to the mall and pick out some glasses?"

Frances shrugged.

"I think it would be fun, don't you, Polly?" Mrs. McAllister asked.

Looking torn between standing up for her friend

and arguing with her friend's mother, Polly said carefully, "I have time if that's what you want to do."

The mall wasn't very far from Dr. Bemish's office. Mrs. McAllister remembered one of the stores advertised it could make glasses in less than an hour. Fifteen minutes later Frances was inside the Frame Farm looking at more frames than she ever knew existed.

Even Mrs. McAllister looked bewildered. "Where do we start?"

Fortunately a good-looking young man came over to help them. Frances noticed that *he* wasn't wearing glasses. "Who are we looking for?" he asked pleasantly.

Polly jerked her thumb in Frances's direction. "Her."

"All right, come this way." As he walked down the aisle, he said, "She's very small. Her frames need to be delicate."

Frances didn't like the idea of this guy talking about her as if she weren't there, but she allowed herself to be led over to a display case of frames.

"Now, how about these." He pulled a pair of blue frames out of the case.

"Try them on, Frances," her mother urged.

Frances put them on, and they slipped down her nose.

"We'd adjust them to her size, of course," the young man informed Mrs. McAllister.

"What do you think?" her mother asked Frances.

She looked in the mirror. In August, Frances had cut her hair way too short. She had been horrified when she looked in the mirror and saw a stranger's face staring back at her. Now the same feeling washed

over her. All she could see was her small face covered with what seemed like enormous blue frames.

"How do you like them?" the salesman asked brightly.

"I don't." She turned to Polly. "You don't like them, do you?" she asked desperately.

"Well, they are kind of . . . blue."

"Perhaps something a little plainer," Mrs. McAllister said to the salesman.

After almost half an hour of trying on all sorts of frames, Frances felt no closer to making a decision than she had when she first put on the blue glasses. However, her mother, the young salesman, and even Polly looked as if they were more than ready for her to pick out something. Anything.

"You said I could get something I liked," she reminded her mother as she put down a pair of horn-rims.

Mrs. McAllister looked as if she was trying to hold on to her temper. It seemed to be slipping out of her grasp anyway. "Many of them looked nice."

"That's really all we have for young people," the salesman said. He eyed a customer who was tapping her foot impatiently. "Maybe you want to think about it for a couple of days."

"Yes," Frances said.

"No," countered her mother. "We need these as soon as possible."

Polly moved away and began trying on sunglasses, peering at herself in a hand mirror.

Frances grabbed some frames made of thin gold wire. "These. I'll take these."

"Are you sure?" Mrs. McAllister asked.

It didn't matter. Frances had already made the decision that she wasn't going to wear them. "These are fine."

The salesman breathed a sigh of relief. "Great. Give me the prescription, and I'll see how much they're going to cost."

Frances and Mrs. McAllister followed him over to the counter. He punched in some figures and then said, "It'll be seventy-five dollars. Plus tax."

"Mom, seventy-five dollars!"

"We'll charge them," Mrs. McAllister said calmly.

"But you hate to charge stuff. You always say if you don't have cash, you shouldn't buy something."

"That may be true for frivolous things. But glasses are a necessity."

Frances knew that her mother wouldn't back down. Even though money was tight, Frances would get her glasses. Now she felt really bad knowing that she had no intention of wearing them. It was just like throwing seventy-five dollars away. Well, Frances thought a little belligerently, she had tried to tell her mother it was a waste of money.

The trio spent the next hour walking around the mall waiting for the glasses to be finished. Frances saw plenty of cute sweaters that she would have preferred spending the money on.

"What color case would you like?" the salesman asked cheerfully.

"It doesn't matter," Frances said. Nobody was going to see it anyway, she thought. Or what was inside.

4

rances hoped that she'd be able to dispose of her glasses before anyone saw her in them, but she had forgotten about her family. All of them knew that she had gone to the eye doctor. And since Mrs. McAllister hadn't been home to fix an early Saturday dinner, they figured that the excursion had led to the Frame Farm. So by the time Frances and her mother arrived home, the rest of the family was waiting around the table for a fashion show.

Mr. McAllister was a sandwich-fixer *extraordinaire*, and he had made a pile of turkey sandwiches for the family's supper. He and Elizabeth and Mike were already eating when Frances and Mrs. McAllister walked in.

"So where are they?" Mr. McAllister asked, wiping his lips with a napkin.

Frances pointed to her pocket.

"Let's see them," Mike said.

"How do they look?" Elizabeth asked.

With her family sitting here staring at her, Frances didn't see how she could avoid doing what they wanted. She stuck her hand in her pocket and pulled out the glasses case. "There," she said, sticking them on her face.

"They look nice, honey," her father said.

Elizabeth looked at her more critically. "I think I might have liked silver a little better."

"I tried on about a million pair," Frances said with exasperation. "This one was the best."

Mike chomped away at his sandwich. "They look okay. I mean, if you have to wear glasses."

"Well, she does," Mrs. McAllister said, taking off her coat, "and I think they look very nice."

Frances went to hang up her coat. Catching sight of herself in the hall mirror, she was taken aback. Was that really her? Frances's hair had grown since the fall, but it was still shorter than she liked. Sometimes she used a headband to pull it back, but then her ears stuck out. Now, wearing her new glasses, she seemed like an entirely different person. And that person, in her opinion, looked pretty silly.

Putting her glasses back in their case, she resolved that that was where they would stay.

By the time she returned to the table, Frances was relieved to see that the topic had turned away from her. But the subject the McAllisters were now discussing was just as upsetting.

"I just don't know how long I can hang on at the store," her father was saying.

"But Daddy, if you don't keep the store what will you do?" Frances asked, sliding into her chair.

"I guess I could try and get a job at the hardware store out at the mall."

"That stinks," Mike said.

"So does not eating or having a roof over our heads," Mr. McAllister replied with a sigh.

"Well, we're not quite ready to give up yet. At least, I'm not," Mrs. McAllister said firmly.

Mr. McAllister smiled a tired smile. "Do you have a plan, dear? Sounds like you do."

"Yes. While I was at the mall waiting for Frances's glasses, I saw lots of Help Wanted signs. I thought I could apply for a job."

"But you already have a job at the real-estate office," Elizabeth pointed out. "And you're studying to get your real-estate license."

"True. But my job's only part-time. I could get another part-time job in one of the shops."

"Oh, Jeannie, that's a lot to take on," Mr. McAllister said. "I don't want you running yourself into the ground."

Frances nibbled at her sandwich. She didn't like to think of her mom being away from home so much. Polly's mother worked full-time, and she was almost never around.

"Of course, if I did that, you kids would have to help out a lot more," Mrs. McAllister said, glancing around the table.

"I'd help out," Elizabeth said eagerly.

Elizabeth could be such a goody-goody sometimes, Frances thought darkly. Oh, she'd be the first one to say she wanted to help, but when the time came to actually do something, she'd disappear.

"I think all of you are old enough now to assume more responsibility around here."

I'm only nine, Frances wanted to say, and I already load the dishwasher and keep my half of the room clean. But instead she just pushed the potato chips around on her plate.

"I hate the idea of you having yet another job," Mr. McAllister said, looking as glum as Frances felt.

His wife patted his hand. "It will just be for a little while. Until business picks up."

When will that be? Frances wondered. As she looked around the table, she could see that she wasn't the only one with that thought in her mind.

As she dragged herself out of bed on Monday morning, Frances didn't know what she should worry about most—all the possible changes going on at her house or making sure that no one saw her in her glasses.

She put on one of her favorite outfits, her jeans and a great orange Save the Whales sweatshirt, hoping that would perk her up a little. Glancing over at Elizabeth, she jealously noted Elizabeth's blond curls and how tall she was. Boy, Frances thought, when looks were parceled out for the McAllister family, Elizabeth must have gotten my share.

"What are you staring at?" Elizabeth asked as she hooked a silver bracelet around her wrist.

"Nothing," Frances said, turning away.

"After you went to bed, I heard Mom say that she was going over to the mall to apply for jobs today."

"Already?"

"Yes. Maybe she'll put me in charge while she's at work," Elizabeth said happily.

"In charge of who? Me?"

"Of course. I can make sure you help with dinner and that your homework gets done . . ."

This plan was sounding worse and worse to Frances.

"What about Mike? You don't think you're going to be in charge of him, too, do you?"

"I should be. He's gotten so weird since he started high school. All he thinks about is Bambi Jones."

Frances was all ears now. "Is that the name of his girlfriend? Bambi?"

Elizabeth nodded, and the girls laughed. "She's a real dear," Elizabeth said, giggling. "Get it?"

"How do you know her name?"

"Her sister is in my class. Besides, I've seen them together in the Sweet Shoppe."

"When?" Frances squealed.

"Yesterday." Elizabeth lowered her voice. "He had his arm around her."

"No!"

Frances flopped down on the bed. "I can't believe any girl would let Mike put his arm around her." Frances sat up. "Around her what?"

"What?" Elizabeth asked, puzzled.

"I mean her waist or her shoulder."

"Shoulder."

"Did he look dumb?"

Elizabeth thought about it. "No. He just looked happy."

Frances pondered the mystery of love. What was it about a girl named Bambi that could make her brother walk around like he was in a dream? For that matter, why did Elizabeth have a crush on Mr. Winnow, of all people? She couldn't imagine getting all worked up over a boy. She couldn't imagine a boy getting all worked up over her, either.

Frances thought about Mike and his girlfriend all

the way to school. It was a much more pleasant topic than any of the other ones on her mind.

"What's with you? You're so quiet." Polly, as usual, was sitting next to her on the bus.

"I was thinking about Mike and his girlfriend, Bambi. I've never seen him act so strange."

"That's what a boyfriend will do," Polly said with disgust.

"You sound like you know all about it."

"I think my mother has a boyfriend."

"No! Who?"

"I don't know. But she's been whispering on the telephone lately."

"That's how it starts," Frances said, nodding wisely. "That's how it started with Mike."

"She was on the phone for about an hour yesterday. And when I asked her who she was talking to, she just smiled and said maybe I'd find out someday."

"Weird."

"It sure is. I know my father has been dating since my parents got divorced, but my mom hasn't. Until now," Polly added with a sigh.

"She should tell you who he is."

"Right. I don't know what the big secret is."

The girls discussed the various possibilities all the way to school. There were no men working at the library, and Polly hadn't heard her mother talking about anyone special.

"Well, I guess I'll find out eventually," Polly said, "but it sure is weird to think some guy likes my mother."

Frances was glad that her parents were happily married. They were too old to start dating, Frances was sure.

The girls walked into their classroom. A strange teacher was sitting at Mr. Winnow's desk.

"Substitute," Polly said with a grin.

Frances immediately felt sorry for the middle-aged woman who was worriedly looking at the lesson plan. Substitutes never had an easy time, but there were always a couple of kids who made their lives miserable. Polly was one of them. Albert Bell was another.

Polly pulled Frances off into a corner. "Let's switch identities."

"What?"

"You be me, and I'll be you."

Frances could feel a nervous twinge in her stomach. "That's silly. She'll catch on. The other kids will tell her."

"Never in a million years."

Frances knew that Polly was right. The kids would probably enjoy the joke. But when she thought about how much trouble they could get into if the substitute found out, Frances felt a little ill.

"Just follow my lead," Polly said confidently.

"I'm Mrs. Sheer," the teacher announced as the bell rang. "Mr. Winnow is taking a personal day today, but he left his lesson plan. Let's start by calling the roll. Maybe I'll remember a few of your names."

Mrs. Sheer went through the A's. Then she called out, "Albert Bell."

Albert stood up. "I'm Albert, and I'm the class monitor."

The class giggled. There was no monitor, and if there had been, it certainly wouldn't have been Albert.

"You are?" Mrs. Sheer asked uncertainly. "What are your responsibilities?"

"Oh, I just help out. Like, do you need any paper?"

Before Mrs. Sheer could answer, Albert went over to the supply cabinet and got out a ream of paper. He plunked it on the desk in front of Mrs. Sheer.

"Well, thank you, but I don't—"

"How about some chalk?" He hurried over to the cabinet and took out a box.

"Albert, I don't need any more supplies, thank you."

"Oh." Albert pasted a disappointed look on his face. He went back to his seat. "Whatever you need, though . . ."

"Yes." Mrs. Sheer continued with the roll call. "Polly Brock?"

Polly looked over in Frances's direction and nodded. Frances looked down at her desk, but she could feel Polly's eyes piercing into her.

"Polly Brock?"

Frances lifted her hand slowly. "Here." A small gasp went around the room. Frances glanced over at Lena, who looked positively frightened. Mrs. Sheer didn't seem to notice; she just went on reading off names. When she said, "Frances McAllister," Polly loudly answered, "Present."

Frances looked at Polly, who was giggling, and then sneaked a peek at Albert. His lip was sticking out, and Frances couldn't tell if he was about to laugh or if he was angry he hadn't thought of a similar trick.

It wasn't long before Albert had a chance to show off again, though. First period was spelling, and the fourth grade was scheduled for a test. It was supposed to be on chapter 9, but as Mrs. Sheer was telling the class to take out their papers, Albert raised his hand. "Mrs. Sheer, our test is on chapter 8."

"Chapter 8? This says chapter 9."

"No, ma'am. It's hard to read Mr. Winnow's writing sometimes, but we're on chapter 8." He looked around the room, daring anyone to challenge him.

Mrs. Sheer peered at the lesson plan. "I suppose this could be an eight." Looking up, she asked, "Chapter 8?"

Several of the boys—and Polly—nodded earnestly.

"All right then, I will test you on chapter 8."

It was the easiest test Frances had ever taken. She had gotten an 80 on the same test last week and had been required to write out the words she had missed ten times each. So Frances was sure she'd get a 100 this time. Too bad Mr. Winnow wouldn't count the results.

Second period was history. Mrs. Sheer had the class read aloud. First she asked Sheila to read. Then it was Polly's turn.

Frances was drawing a flower on the margin of her history book.

"Polly, where are you?"

Frances suddenly felt a spitball hit her in the arm. "Hey," she said, looking up. Albert, one row over, was grinning at her.

"You're Polly, aren't you?" Mrs. Sheer asked.

"Uh, yes."

"Well, please read."

Frances read.

"Young lady, will you pay attention?"

Frances looked up to see Mrs. Sheer glaring at Polly.

"I can't help it, Mrs. Sheer. He"—she pointed at Albert—"was throwing spitballs at me."

"Prove it!" Albert said, his voice quivering with indignation.

Polly picked up the spitball. "What's this?"

"You can't prove I threw it."

"Frances, Albert, please!"

Frances cringed to hear her name being spoken in such an angry tone of voice.

"And Albert, you, the class monitor, being so disruptive. I'm surprised." Now the class burst into laughter in earnest. If anything was *not* surprising, it was Albert being disruptive.

"He isn't a monitor," Polly said scornfully. "He's the worst kid in the class."

"And she's not Frances McAllister," Albert cut in quickly. "She's Polly Brock."

Mrs. Sheer looked confused. "Then who's Frances?"

Albert pointed a finger at Frances. "She is."

5

"I'm very disappointed in you, class," Mr. Winnow said, a dour look on his face. "I take one day off, and you children can't be trusted to be on your best behavior."

In his hand was a two-page report from Mrs. Sheer detailing the class's shenanigans. The names Frances, Polly, and Albert figured prominently. Frances had never seen Mr. Winnow look so upset.

"You're all getting extra homework, and of course your spelling test—on chapter 8—won't be figured into your grade. We'll have our test on chapter 9 in a few minutes. Polly, Albert, and Frances, I'd like to see you before you go to lunch."

While the rest of the class filtered out into the hall at lunchtime, Albert, Frances, and Polly shuffled up to Mr. Winnow's desk. He folded his arms in front of him and frowned. "Frankly, Albert and Polly, I'm not surprised that you're involved in this—but you, Frances?"

Frances felt horrible. Mr. Winnow was right. This

wasn't like her. In fact, she had almost lost her temper at Polly over the whole affair yesterday after school. "You should have left me out of it," she'd said grumpily as she sipped some hot chocolate at Polly's house.

"You could have said no."

"But then you would have been mad at me."

Polly shrugged. "I would have gotten over it. After all, if I told you to jump off a bridge, would you do it?"

This statement made Frances angry. It was the same thing her mother said when she thought Frances was being overly influenced by somebody. "No way."

"So you shouldn't have done this either if you didn't want to."

Polly was right, Frances supposed. But the sight of her friend happily drinking her hot chocolate and eating a cookie as though there were nothing wrong was driving her crazy. Maybe Polly was used to being in trouble, but she wasn't. It was also very hard for her to tell somebody she was mad at them, especially her best friend. Nevertheless, Frances screwed up her courage. "I'm never going to go along with any of your plans again. Not if they're stupid, like this one was."

Frances waited for Polly to shoot back a sarcastic answer. But Polly was so easygoing, all she said was, "Fine. Try to keep *me* from doing stupid stuff too, okay?"

Frances had to laugh. She and Polly were so different. They fit together pretty well, though. "I'll try, but that's a big job, Polly Brock."

After the girls had eaten their snack, Frances convinced herself that their behavior really wasn't so bad. But now, standing in front of Mr. Winnow, she began to feel awful all over again, especially since he seemed so disappointed in her.

"I'm sorry," she said quietly.

"How about you two? Are you sorry, too?"

Polly and Albert both nodded, but Mr. Winnow looked as if he wasn't sure he believed them.

"Your punishment is to stay after school. I will have an assignment for you then."

"But I have a ballet lesson after school," Frances said, her voice trembling a little.

"Then you'll have to miss it, or be late for it. Would you like me to call your mother and tell her?"

"No." Missing her lesson was horrible, but if she could keep her family out of this, it would be worth it.

"Then I'll see the three of you after school."

As soon as Mr. Winnow left the room, Albert raised a fist in the air. "No stupid ballet. Yes!"

Frances didn't see how this day could get much worse. Not only was she missing ballet, she was missing a class that would have been Albert-free.

But things spiraled downward even further after the last bell when the trio sat at their desks after the rest of the class had been dismissed.

"All right," Mr. Winnow said. "I want you to take out a piece of paper and write a letter to Mrs. Sheer apologizing for your behavior. Use both sides, please."

It was a horrible assignment. After Frances wrote that she was sorry, she couldn't think of anything else to say. She had only used up about two lines of the first page.

She glanced out the window, and she noticed how hard it was to make out the individual branches of the trees. Mr. Winnow must have followed her gaze.

"Frances," he said, "I've been meaning to ask you. Has your mother taken you to the eye doctor?"

Frances saw Albert looking at her. "Yes," she said in a whisper.

"Did he prescribe glasses for you?"

She glanced at Albert. "Uh, yes."

Albert smirked and mimed a pair of glasses with his fingers, which he put over his eyes. Then he crossed them.

Mr. Winnow didn't notice. "Then why didn't I see you wearing them today?"

Frances hesitated. "I forgot them at home." It wasn't a total lie. She *had* left them in her underwear drawer.

"Well, don't forget again."

"No, Mr. Winnow."

Darn, Frances thought. Now Albert knew that she wore glasses. Well, there was nothing she could do about it now. She picked up her pen and tried to finish her letter to Mrs. Sheer. She wrote very large and figured out how to say she was sorry about ten different ways.

When she was finished, she brought her paper up to Mr. Winnow. He looked it over and said, "I guess this will do. You are dismissed."

Frances looked at the clock over Mr. Winnow's head. Maybe there was still time to get to ballet. She caught Polly's eye and mouthed, "I'm going to dance class." Polly nodded and went back to her writing.

Frances wasn't worried about Albert showing up at Miss Leticia's. As she passed by him, she noticed that he was still on the first side of his piece of paper. He seemed to be drawing a picture of a shark, although what that had to do with his apology, Frances couldn't imagine.

She ran practically the whole way to Miss Leticia's, but the class was almost over when she arrived.

"I'm sorry, Miss Leticia," Frances said breathlessly as she came into the studio. "I had to stay after school."

Miss Leticia frowned. "Frances, if you're going to have the lead in the dance, you have to attend practice."

"It won't happen again," Frances swore.

"All right. Class dismissed."

Frances turned to go home, but Miss Leticia stopped her. "Frances, I'd like to talk to you for a moment."

"Yes, Miss Leticia?"

"Did Albert have to stay after school today as well?"

Frances didn't know what to say. Miss Leticia was his aunt, after all. She'd probably tell his mother, and then Albert would be angry with her. Miss Leticia was waiting for an answer, however. "Yes, Albert was there too."

"Well, I won't ask you why you had to stay after school. Just remember we need you here in class."

"Oh, I know," Frances said fervently. "And I've been practicing my part at home."

"That's good. The day of the recital will be here before we know it."

"Is it going to be here at the studio?" Frances asked shyly.

"Yes. I'm going to advertise it in the paper. I know friends and family will be here, but I'd like some other people to attend too. I wish more people shopped downtown. We might draw in some of those people as well."

"My father complains about that, too," Frances said. "He's having a terrible time at our hardware store because nobody shops on Main Street."

"Maybe if all the merchants got together, we could do something about that," Miss Leticia said thoughtfully. "I'll have to think about it."

Miss Leticia's words made Frances hopeful. She wasn't sure what her ballet teacher could actually do to improve business in town, but she seemed pretty smart. Maybe she could come up with some ideas. Frances could hardly wait to tell her father Miss Leticia was working on it. Perhaps that would cheer him up.

But when Frances arrived home, there was more bad news waiting for her. At least, *she* thought it was bad news. Her mother had found a job.

"I'm going to work at Linens Plus as a salesclerk," Mrs. McAllister was telling the family as Frances walked through the door. "It's from three to nine three days a week and every other Saturday."

She looked pretty pleased, Frances thought. Elizabeth did too. But her father and Mike didn't seem too thrilled by the news.

"You're going to need someone to be in charge, right, Mom?" Elizabeth said hopefully.

Oh, no, Frances thought. Here she goes.

Mrs. McAllister looked puzzled. "Your father will be in charge when he gets home."

"But until then," Elizabeth insisted.

"Well, of course I want all of you to help get dinner ready. And do your regular cleaning-up chores. If there are any problems, go to Mike."

"Mike?" Elizabeth cried.

"Who else? Mike always baby-sits when you're home alone."

Mike made a face at his sister. "Yeah, and you'd better do what I say, baby."

"See, Mom? See how he's going to act? I think I should be in charge."

Frances turned away to hang up her coat. She knew one thing for sure—nobody was going to put her in charge.

Mr. McAllister finally spoke up. "This is a silly argument. I think you're all old enough to take care of yourselves. You know what you're supposed to do. Naturally, if there's some kind of problem, Mike, as the oldest, will make the decisions. But I don't expect situations like that to come up very often. At least, I hope they won't."

Neither Mike nor Elizabeth seemed very happy with this plan, but it was a good solution for Frances. Her dad was on record as saying they all could take care of themselves. That meant her, too.

In celebration of her new job, Mrs. McAllister had

brought home a bucket of chicken with all the trimmings. It had been a long time since the family had eaten a takeout meal. As she was dishing out the mashed potatoes, Mrs. McAllister asked the question Frances had been dreading. "How was your ballet lesson, Frances?"

Frances looked down at her biscuit. "I got there late."

To Frances's relief, her mother didn't ask why. "Anything interesting happen?"

This was the perfect opportunity to tell her parents what Miss Leticia said about bringing more business to Main Street. But no one seemed very excited by the ballet teacher's words.

"She's got the right idea," Mr. McAllister said, "but how exactly is she going to do that?"

Mrs. McAllister passed around more biscuits. "What could possibly bring people to town in the middle of winter, with half the shops closed?"

Frances was disappointed in their reaction. "I don't know, but maybe if we all thought about it, we'd come up with something."

"I've done nothing *but* think about it," Mr. McAllister reminded her. "I wish I had an idea, but I don't."

"Oh, well, the recital will be a big success, I'm sure," Elizabeth said.

"Why?" Mike asked. "Because you're going to be dancing?"

"That's one of the reasons," she informed him haughtily.

"Sounds like a good reason not to go." Mike laughed.

"Children, children," Mrs. McAllister said, rubbing her head. "How can I leave you alone while I'm working if you can't even get along at the dinner table?"

Mike and Elizabeth had the good grace to look ashamed.

"Your mother's right," Mr. McAllister said. "Now, more than ever, we've all got to pull together."

After dinner, Mrs. McAllister drove Frances over to Polly's house. Usually Frances wasn't allowed out on a school night, but she, Polly, and Lena were working on a geography report together, so special permission had been granted for a meeting.

As the girls worked, Polly and Frances filled Lena in on what had gone on that afternoon.

"But the worst part was when Mr. Winnow mentioned my glasses. Now Albert knows all about them."

"Oh, he wasn't even paying any attention," Polly said.

"Yes, he *was*," Frances insisted. "He looked right at me, pretended he was wearing glasses, and made a face."

Polly colored in one of the oceans of the world. "That figures."

"I'm just not going to wear them."

"But you have to sometime," Lena said.

"No, I don't," Frances replied grimly.

Lena fiddled with her pencil. "It isn't smart to walk around being unable to see, Frances."

"How much are you supposed to be wearing them, anyway?" Polly asked.

Frances made a face. "The doctor said as much as possible, except when I'm doing close work like reading."

"Do you wear them at home?" Lena wanted to know.

"Not really."

"Has your mom noticed?"

Frances shook her head. "Everyone at home is so worried about my dad's store, they don't think about much else. My mother got another part-time job today," she said softly.

"Oh, it's not so bad when your mother works," Polly informed her. "You'll get used to it."

"Maybe. But I sure wish there was some way I could help. Miss Leticia thinks there should be more business on Main Street, too." Then Frances told them what Miss Leticia had said that afternoon.

Polly stretched out on her den floor. "Too bad everything happens here in the summer."

"Winter is pretty dead everywhere, I guess," Frances said.

"Not in Milwaukee. They have a big winter carnival there that's great." Polly had lived in Milwaukee before she moved to Lake Lister.

"That sounds like fun," Lena said.

"Oh, it is. There is ice-skating and ice sculpture contests. It's on the lake, and lots of people come out for it."

"We have a lake," Frances said thoughtfully.

"Yeah, but we don't have the same amount of

people Milwaukee does. We have about a fiftieth of them. Hey, want to have something to eat?" Polly asked. "We're almost done with this geography stuff."

The girls went into the kitchen then, but Frances filed away in the back of her mind what Polly had said about the winter carnival.

Lying in bed that night, she thought about it again. Lake Lister's main street bordered the lake. If there was some big event out there, it might bring a lot of people into the town. But a carnival like Polly was talking about was a big undertaking. It would take a lot of planning. Shy little Frances McAllister couldn't do anything like that. Or could she?

6

frances got up the next morning as sleepy as when she had crawled into bed. She'd had weird dreams all night. A winter carnival was going on, and lots of tourists were roaming around the town. Mr. McAllister was selling all of them snow shovels, which they used to crazily toss snow everywhere.

Albert was in the dream, too. He was wearing a tutu and a pair of glasses. During the ice sculpture contest he kept carving large sharks.

"Ugh!" Frances said at the memory as she leaped out of bed.

Elizabeth was just turning over. "Don't make so much noise," she said with a groan.

As roommates, Frances and Elizabeth couldn't have been more different. Besides the neatness factor, Frances almost always woke up in a happy mood, while Elizabeth could hardly be coaxed out of bed at all. She hated noise in the morning, so Frances had to tiptoe around until her sister got up.

This morning, though, Frances didn't make any effort to be quiet. She was in a hurry to start the day. If only she could figure out who would be the best person to tell her idea to about a winter carnival.

In the shower and as she dressed, Frances tried to think how to put her plan into action. Of course, she could share her idea with her father, but somehow she knew he wouldn't pay much attention to it. Neither would her mom. They both were so caught up in the family's problems that they would just think Frances was being silly. Who knew? Maybe she was.

She saved her usual seat on the bus for Polly. But when the bus stopped at Polly's corner, she didn't get on. That was strange. Usually Frances would have gotten a call if Polly wasn't coming to school. Albert, however, did get on, and he plopped down on the seat next to her.

Frances took a book out of her backpack and pretended to start reading.

"Where's Polly-Want-a-Cracker?"

"I don't know," Frances mumbled, not looking up.

"Some punishment we had yesterday, huh?"

What was this? Albert trying to make conversation? Frances buried her head in the book, but then she just had to ask him something. "Was that a shark you were drawing in your apology letter?"

Albert grinned. "Sure was."

"But what was it doing there?"

"I was drawing her an apology. I told her I wanted to do something nice for her. To show her I'm not such a bad kid."

"So you drew a shark?"

Albert popped a piece of gum in his mouth. "Sure.

I'm a talented artist. She's lucky to get an Albert Bell original.''

Frances rolled her eyes. "Oh, right."

"Mr. Winnow said it was a nice thing to do." Albert actually seemed hurt.

Frances couldn't quite believe that she was sitting here talking back to Albert Bell, just the way Polly did. She was beginning to feel very powerful when Albert looked at her and said, "Where's your specs?"

"Specs?" Frances squeaked.

"Yeah, you know, glasses."

All Frances's newfound confidence began oozing out of her.

"In my backpack."

"When are we going to get a look-see?"

You? Frances thought. Never.

"Frances Four-Eyes," Albert began singing, "loves all the boys . . .''

The kids in the seat in front of them turned around.

"Will you be quiet!" Frances snapped.

"Aw, I was just kidding."

Frances pretended great interest in her book.

"Are you going to wear them at the recital?"

"What?"

"Your glasses. You'll need them to dance, right?"

Frances hadn't thought about that. She was supposed to wear her glasses as much as possible, but there was no way she was going to be caught in glasses while she was dancing. Why, there had probably never been a dancer wearing glasses in the whole history of ballet. "I won't need them when I dance."

"Well, if you need them, you'd better wear them. I don't want you tripping all over me."

Frances couldn't wait to get off the bus. Polly was waiting for her in the schoolyard. "Where were you?" Frances demanded.

"I overslept, so my mother had to give me a ride."

"Albert sat down next to me," Frances told her disgustedly.

"Ugh!"

"Ugh is right. He was teasing me about my glasses."

"Forget about him," Polly advised as they walked to the door. "If he starts up with you again, we'll just get on him about his hair and those ugly freckles of his."

Polly was a very satisfying best friend, Frances thought. She always knew just the right thing to say.

There were still a few moments before the bell rang. Frances decided she wanted to bounce her idea about a winter carnival off of Polly. "I was thinking about something last night."

Polly rubbed her hands up and down her arms. It was cold. "Yeah? What?"

"Remember what you said about a winter carnival?"

"Sure."

"Maybe we could have one here." All the thoughts she had had since last night began tumbling out. "If we could get people into town, maybe they would shop on Main Street, and if they did, they might keep coming back."

Polly looked at her with approval. "Hey. That's a pretty good idea." Then Polly frowned. "But we couldn't organize it. We're just kids."

"I know. That's the problem."

The bell rang, and the girls hurried into the warm school. "We'd have to get some grownups interested," Polly said.

"Maybe Miss Leticia."

"Yeah. But she couldn't do it alone."

As she hung up her coat and went to her seat, Frances tried to tell herself a winter carnival was still a good idea. But she didn't have the faintest idea of how to get it off the ground.

Once the class got settled, Mr. Winnow said, "I want to talk to you about our community service project."

The fourth grade had decided on Polly's suggestion of a book drive. Everyone was going to clean out their bookshelves and bring in their old books for the library's book sale.

As Mr. Winnow roamed the room and talked about bringing in old books, Frances started thinking about the carnival again. Now would be a good time to bring it up, Frances realized, but she was a little hesitant to do so. The class already had a project. Would anyone be interested in another one?

Frances looked over at Polly, who must have been thinking the same thing. She gestured for Frances to raise her hand.

Frances had never felt so timid in her life. She never thought of herself as the kind of person who had good ideas. No, she was always the one who waited for somebody else to think up plans. Then a picture of her normally cheerful dad sitting sadly at the kitchen table flashed into her mind. If she didn't get up and at least offer her idea, there was no way she could help him.

"Yes, Frances?" Mr. Winnow was looking at her curiously. Somehow her hand had risen, but she wasn't saying anything.

Frances cleared her throat. "I have an idea of something we could do for a community service project. I mean another one."

Haltingly she told the class about how bad business was on Main Street. Then she told them about the winter carnival in Milwaukee.

Polly raised her hand. "I've been to lots of them. There are ice-skating races and snowman-building contests. There's a snowball-throwing competition, too. And booths with cookies and hot chocolate and cider," she added.

"Well, maybe we could do something like that here," Frances said. "It would be fun for everybody, and maybe more people would come into town."

Frances had been looking at the floor while she was speaking, but now she raised her head. She was surprised to see how interested everyone seemed in her idea.

"Well, Frances," Mr. Winnow said, "you certainly have been thinking about this matter, I see. It would be a big undertaking, though. Bigger than anything this fourth-grade class could handle. But it would certainly be interesting to be a part of it. What do you think, class?"

There was a flurry of raised hands. "Yes, Tammi?" Mr. Winnow said.

"I think a winter carnival would be really cool. It's so *bor*-ing here in the winter."

"Yes, it would be cool. It might be very cold," Mr. Winnow agreed, smiling at his small joke. "But do you think it would help Lake Lister?"

Jamie Gilbert raised his hand. "My dad works at Crawford's Department Store, and he says business is bad. He's afraid the store is going to close."

"So some kind of activity may help business. Lena?"

"The booths would make money. We could donate it to charity."

"That would certainly benefit the community," Mr. Winnow said approvingly. "Polly, do you have something else to say?"

"I think a winter carnival would be great. Just because we're only in the fourth grade doesn't mean we can't have good ideas." She threw a smile in Frances's direction.

Albert spoke up. "If this thing gets off the ground, everyone will know how awesome Mr. Winnow's class is."

There was a lot more discussion after that. Mr. Winnow just sat back and let them talk. Even though the class knew it would be hard to organize something like a winter carnival, most of the kids still wanted to see how far they could go with it.

"Frances, since this was your idea, what do you want to do about it?" Mr. Winnow asked.

Frances was amazed at the class's enthusiasm. Now she felt as if she had to keep them interested. "I guess

I can talk to Miss Leticia, my dance teacher. She said she wanted to get more people downtown."

"That's a good idea." Mr. Winnow nodded approvingly. "I can talk to the principal. Let's see what she has to suggest."

Mr. Winnow went on to math, and though Frances opened her book to the right page, she really wasn't paying attention. She kept replaying her little speech over and over again in her mind. She couldn't believe she'd had the nerve to say anything.

At lunch both Polly and Lena said they were impressed.

"You explained it so well," Lena said, smiling.

"I couldn't have done it better myself," Polly said proudly.

"Well, you did help, and I appreciate it. Now I just have to talk to Miss Leticia. Can either of you come with me?"

Lena couldn't. She had to do her homework, as usual. Polly said she'd walk over with her but added, "I'll meet you at the Sweet Shoppe after you're done."

"Why not just come in with me and help me explain?"

Polly licked some mustard from her finger. "For one thing, you don't need me. For another, that dance studio gives me the willies."

"Do you think Miss Leticia will grab you and make you rejoin the class?" Frances teased.

"Let's put it like this: I'm not taking any chances."

After school, Frances and Polly went downtown. Polly turned off at the Sweet Shoppe while Frances hurried on to the dance studio. Elizabeth had her tap lesson today, but not until four. Frances hoped that if she arrived early enough, Miss Leticia would be free.

She was just finishing up with the preschoolers when Frances walked through the door. For a moment Miss Leticia looked confused. "Frances, it's not your day, is it?"

"No. But I need to talk to you," Frances said shyly.

Miss Leticia glanced at the slim gold watch she wore. "I have a few minutes. Come into my office."

Frances had never been inside Miss Leticia's office before. There were photographs of dancers on the walls and several books about ballet lying on the desk. Frances thought the office was very cozy.

"So tell me what I can do for you."

Frances took a deep breath. "Remember yesterday you were talking about the recital and how nice it would be to have lots of people come?"

Miss Leticia nodded.

"Well, I think I have an idea." Quickly Frances outlined her plan. She expected Miss Leticia to stop her at any moment and tell her she was being silly, but Miss Leticia just kept nodding as Frances talked.

Tapping her long fingernails together, the dance teacher said thoughtfully, "Very interesting."

"Do you think it might work?"

"I don't know, Frances. It would be a heck of a lot of work, and we wouldn't have very long to get it organized. But we're in luck. All the merchants in the county get together once a month for the Chamber of Commerce dinner."

"I know. My father goes to that."

"It's tonight. I could bring up the plan then. I don't know if anyone would be interested, but I'll ask."

"Oh, thank you!"

"No, thank *you*. But now I must get back to class. We'll see what happens." Miss Leticia put her arm around Frances's shoulder and walked her out of the office and into the studio. Elizabeth was just passing through on her way to the dressing room. She did a double take.

"Hi, Elizabeth." Frances's tone was almost bored. She acted as if she and Miss Leticia palled around together every day of the week.

"What are you doing here?"

"Uh . . ."

"Frances and I were just having a chat," Miss Leticia cut in smoothly.

Frances knew Elizabeth wanted to say "What about?" but didn't have the nerve.

"Your sister is quite clever, you know."

So there, Elizabeth, Frances wanted to say. Instead she tried to look modest.

"Oh, sure, I know," Elizabeth mumbled. She moved as fast as she could into the dressing room.

Frances couldn't have been more pleased.

"I'll let you know what happens, dear," Miss Leticia said as she walked Frances to the door.

"Thanks, Miss Leticia." Frances really meant it.

"You're very welcome."

Even though the snow was piled high on the ground, Frances almost danced her way over to the Sweet Shoppe. She peered in the window and saw Polly

diving into what looked like her second piece of pie—
one empty plate was already in front of her.

"Hi," Frances sang as she walked through the door.
"How did it go?"

"Great!"

Pops Butterfield, the owner of the Sweet Shoppe,
came up to Frances as she slid into the booth. "You
look pretty happy," he commented.

It struck Frances that Pops might be a good person
to tell about her plan. Even though he usually had
lots of business because he had the best ice cream in
town, he would probably like more. "Pops," she began, "did you ever hear of a winter carnival?"

She finished the hot chocolate Pops brought over
and was done talking at the same time. Pops looked
just as pleased as Miss Leticia. "You might be on to
something there, Little One."

Pops had called her Little One forever. She didn't
mind when he made a reference about her size. "I'll
tell you what," he continued. "I think I'll call over to
Miss Leticia's. Maybe we can work together on this."

Polly and Frances looked at each other and smiled.

"What about your dad? Doesn't he want to get in
on this?"

"I—I haven't told him yet."

"Why, I thought he'd be the first person you'd talk
to."

Frances shook her head. "He's been kind of
down . . ."

Pops nodded wisely. "Might have just dismissed
the idea. Better to come from one of us."

Frances was glad Pops understood.

"Say," Polly said, "maybe we should go talk to my mom too. She's going to that Chamber of Commerce thing tonight."

"Why don't you?" Pops agreed. "Your mom's an excellent speaker. She can convince a lot of people of a lot of things."

"Don't I know it," Polly said, making a face. "She convinces me to make my bed every morning."

A light trickle of snow was falling as the girls made their way over to the library. Polly was having dinner with Frances since her mother would be busy tonight. Mrs. Brock could drop them off at Frances's house on the way to the Chamber of Commerce meeting.

Mrs. Brock, as the library director, was often in her office, but sometimes she sat out at the reference desk like the other librarians. She looked a lot like Polly, with the same dark corkscrew curls and dancing brown eyes.

Today she was helping a patron, but they looked more like they were sharing a joke than sharing some information. Mrs. Brock was laughing as she pointed out a line in a book to the man standing in front of her. It took Frances a second to realize that this wasn't just any man, however. Polly noticed it too.

"Look who my mom is talking to," Polly said, elbowing Frances in the ribs.

"I know. Mr. Winnow."

7

" They look mighty cozy," Polly said, narrowing her eyes.

Frances had to admit they did. When Mr. Winnow turned around and saw them standing there, he also looked something else—guilty.

"Hello, girls," he said heartily. Mrs. Brock gave them a small smile.

Polly didn't say anything, and for once Frances had to do the speaking for both of them. "Mrs. Brock, we wanted to talk to you about this idea I had."

"For the winter carnival? Paul . . . uh, Mr. Winnow was just telling me all about it."

Polly nudged Frances ever so slightly again. Frances knew what that nudge meant—she calls him Paul!

"I think it's a very good idea," Mrs. Brock continued. "Have you told anyone else about it?"

"Miss Leticia is going to mention it at the Chamber of Commerce meeting. Pops Butterfield knows about it, too."

"Fine. The more people who will speak up for it,

the better." There was an awkward silence. Mrs. Brock and Mr. Winnow both looked as if they were trying to think of something else to say. Finally Mrs. Brock checked her watch. "If you girls would like to get some books, I'll be able to drive you to Frances's house in a little while."

"We'd rather walk," Polly said.

Frances looked at her friend in amazement. Polly hated to walk. She'd rather ride any day.

"Isn't it starting to snow out there?" Mrs. Brock asked.

"That's okay. It's not falling very hard. Come on, Frances, let's go." Polly headed toward the door without a good-bye.

There was nothing for Frances to do but follow along. "Thanks, Mrs. Brock," she called over her shoulder. "Bye, Mr. Winnow."

As soon as they were out of earshot, Polly said, "I bet Mr. Winnow's the guy she's been seeing. That's why it's been such a big secret."

Frances could see Polly was upset. They stepped outside. The snow was falling much harder now. "Mr. Winnow could have been there for any reason. He is a teacher, after all."

"*Our* teacher," Polly said grimly. "No, it all makes sense. Every time my mother talks to her mystery man on the phone, she looks kind of embarrassed when she hangs up."

"Well, what if she *is* dating Mr. Winnow?" Frances asked as they trudged along. "He's a nice guy."

"It's too weird." Polly stopped in her tracks. "What

if she married him? My teacher would be my step-father!"

"I think you're getting a little ahead of yourself. Come on, keep walking. It's freezing."

Polly started to move. "It sure is."

"Why didn't you let us take a ride with your mother?"

Polly was quiet for a moment. "I wasn't ready to be with her. I don't know what I'd say. What do you think I should say?"

"I wouldn't get upset about it yet."

"Sure, because it's not your mother who's going out with our teacher."

Frances had to smile at that thought. Mrs. Brock was a lot younger than her mother. Mrs. McAllister and Mr. Winnow would make a pretty strange couple.

By the time they arrived at Frances's house the snow was falling in earnest. They were covered with it when they walked through the back door.

Elizabeth was already home, and she frowned at them as they took off their wet coats. "Where have you two been?"

"What do you mean?" Frances asked.

"You should have gotten supper started."

It was Frances's night to make the salad, but she had forgotten all about it.

"Dad's going to that meeting, and Mom's working an extra evening at Linens Plus," Elizabeth continued. "So tonight I'm in charge," she added importantly.

Frances went to the sink and washed her hands. "Who said? Where's Mike?"

"He's not back yet either."

Polly giggled. "So until we got here, you were just in charge of yourself."

"Very funny," Elizabeth said, scowling. "And just what were you doing at Miss Leticia's, by the way?"

Frances didn't like Elizabeth's bossy attitude. She had intended to tell her, but now she made a face and said, "None of your beeswax."

"Oh, grow up! Anyway, where are your glasses, Frances? Aren't you supposed to be wearing them?"

"Elizabeth, you're not my boss. Leave me alone."

"I'll tell Mom you weren't cooperating."

Frances could see a big fight erupting. She figured that Elizabeth was mad because she and Miss Leticia had looked so chummy. Well, let Elizabeth be mad if that's what she wanted. She was going to be even angrier when she found out that Frances had come up with an idea that just might turn everything around for the McAllisters.

But before Frances could launch into a description of her afternoon, Mike lumbered into the kitchen. His jacket and hat were covered with snow, too.

"Oh, Mike, we're so glad you're home," Polly said with mock seriousness. "Now you can be in charge of us."

"I don't want to be in charge of anybody. I just want dinner. Is it ready?"

"Mom's not coming home," Elizabeth said shortly. "We're making it."

Mike shook his head. "Great. Then let's get on with it. I'm starved."

First though, they had to argue about what to have.

"I have a new recipe I thought I would try." Elizabeth waved a crumpled piece of paper that had been sitting on the counter. "Hamburger pie."

"Ugh," Frances and Polly said in unison.

Mike grabbed the paper and studied the picture. "Looks like dog food."

"Mike!" Elizabeth took it out of his hands.

"We're having frozen pizza," Mike said decisively.

Frances and Polly cheered.

"All right," Elizabeth said stiffly, knowing when she was defeated. "But we've got to have salad with it."

Frances didn't know if Elizabeth was insisting on salad because she really wanted it or because she didn't want Frances to get out of doing some work.

"Fine," Mike said. "Frances makes the salad, Polly sets the table, and you take care of the pizza."

"What about you?" Elizabeth asked indignantly.

"I eat it," Mike called as he headed upstairs.

"I'm telling Mom on him," Elizabeth muttered as she took an extra-large pepperoni and sausage pizza from the freezer.

"Oh, what's the point? Mom will just be upset because she'll think we're not getting along, and Mike will do whatever he wants anyway," said Frances.

"I suppose you're right." Elizabeth turned on the oven with a vengeance. "I'm the only one who ever takes anything seriously around here anyway."

Frances and Polly exchanged glances. This might be a good time to show Elizabeth that she wasn't the only one who took things seriously. Frances smiled at her sister sweetly. "Guess what I've been doing this afternoon, Elizabeth?"

By the time Frances had finished telling Elizabeth and Mike all that had happened, dinner was just about over. It had been one of the nicest dinner hours Frances could remember. First she got to see the expressions of amazement on the faces of her brother and sister. Then there was Polly, who kept saying, "Frances was great. You should have seen her. Everybody was so impressed."

"So that's what you were doing at Miss Leticia's," Elizabeth finally said.

Polly answered for her. "Yes, and Miss Leticia was so impressed."

"We get the message," Mike said. "Do you really think this will come off?"

"I don't know," Frances said a little more quietly now. It was fun blowing her own horn, but if everything fell through, she'd wind up looking pretty silly.

"Well, something should happen with it," Mike said. "It's a good idea. Sounds like fun, too."

"Really, Mike?" It wasn't often her brother praised her.

"Heck, the rest of us just sat here worrying about the hardware store. At least you're trying to do something about it."

Even Elizabeth added her congratulations. "Frances, this could be really neat. And if a lot of people come to a carnival, think of how many will show up at our recital."

Frances did start to think about it. If lots of people came to the recital, that meant lots of people would watch her dance. Dancing the lead in their story-ballet, no less, with Albert Bell right beside her. Frances stared off into space. She had had a part in the Christmas show at school, and things hadn't gone too badly. But dancing with Albert. That was something else.

Elizabeth, on the other hand, was thrilled at the prospect of people filling Lake Lister, all with one purpose as she saw it—to watch her tapping away.

"Maybe a talent scout from Milwaukee or even Chicago will be there—"

"On the prowl for an eleven-year-old tap-dancer." Mike snorted back his laughter.

"There might be," Elizabeth said, hurt.

"Don't count on it." Mike pushed away from the table. "I guess it's time for you girls to clean up."

Frances, Elizabeth, and Polly might have their disagreements, but the sight of Mike about to leave the kitchen with a mess on the table united them.

"Hey, wait a minute!" Elizabeth cried.

"You've got to do something around here," Frances added.

"I am. I'm taking care of you guys."

The girls howled at that.

"I think you should clear the table," Polly said.

"You have no opinion, you're just a guest."

"Do you want me to have to tell Mom that you didn't do *anything*?" Elizabeth asked, ready this time to make good on her threat. "Nothing at all but *pretend* to take care of us."

This stopped Mike. He knew Mrs. McAllister wouldn't like to hear that report. "Aw, all right. I guess I can clear the table."

Elizabeth smirked. "See, I am in charge."

Frances, with Polly's help, loaded the dishwasher. Once the kitchen was straightened up, the girls went upstairs to Frances's bedroom.

Snowflake was sleeping on top of the bed. Frances picked her up and gave her a kiss on the head. Slowly the kitten opened her eyes and yawned a tiny yawn.

"Should we get started on our homework?" Frances asked, putting the still sleepy kitten back on the bed.

"I guess," Polly replied listlessly.

"Mr. Winnow wants our English compositions by tomorrow."

Polly flopped down on the floor. She crossed her legs Indian style and studied her hands. "I don't feel like doing anything for him."

Frances really felt Polly was getting upset over nothing. "You don't even know if Mr. Winnow's the guy. And even if he is, you're not going to help anything by not doing your homework."

That comment made Polly look up with interest. "Hey, maybe I can get good grades without doing anything. He wouldn't want to upset my mother, right?"

It was just like Polly to jump to weird conclusions. Frances merely said, "Let's just finish our compositions. We can worry about Mr. Winnow and your mom some other time."

"That's easy for you to say." But Polly tore a piece of paper out of Frances's notebook and began writing.

The phone rang twice while they were working. The first time it was Mrs. McAllister. Elizabeth came upstairs to tell Frances their mother was going to be late.

"Why? The store closes at nine."

"They asked Mom to do some overtime in the stockroom, and she said yes."

Frances didn't like her mother working such long hours. Maybe it was selfish, but she was used to having her home at night, and she missed that.

The second call was from Mrs. Brock. Polly took it in Mr. and Mrs. McAllister's bedroom. Frances couldn't wait until she got back.

"What's happening?" Frances demanded.

"Oh, they've just gotten through the dinner part," Polly said. "They haven't even started the business meeting yet. That's why my mom called. She talked to your dad. He said it would be okay if I slept over."

"Great," Frances said. She and Elizabeth had a rule. Whenever one of their friends slept over, the friend got to use the other bed, leaving the leftover sister to sleep in the basement guest room. Neither of the girls particularly liked the room, but they both knew they'd be called on to sleep in it, so they didn't make a fuss. Still, Elizabeth wouldn't be happy to go down there on a school night. Considering her bossy behavior at dinner, Frances couldn't wait to tell her.

"Did you say anything about Mr. Winnow?" Frances continued.

"Nope."

"Why not?"

"I'll talk to her when we're alone." Polly's face took on a hard, tight expression. It made Frances feel sorry for her friend.

The next morning, Frances woke up before the alarm went off. She looked over at the other bed, where Polly was still lightly snoring. Creeping quietly so as not to wake her, Frances threw on her robe and went downstairs. Usually her parents were up early, having their first cup of coffee.

There they were at the kitchen table, and they looked happy for a change. Frances could feel her heart starting to beat a little faster.

Her dad glanced up and saw her. "Frances McAllister," he said a little formally.

Then he stuck his arms out. "Come here and give your old dad a big hug."

8

frances spent one of the most satisfactory hours of her life sitting down in the warm kitchen having breakfast with her parents.

They were so proud of her.

"Why, when Miss Leticia told the Chamber of Commerce about the winter carnival and then said the idea came from you, I nearly fell out of my chair," Mr. McAllister said.

"Why didn't you tell us about it, honey?" her mother asked as she got some milk from the refrigerator.

"I don't know. You guys seemed so worried. I thought you might think the whole thing was silly."

Mr. McAllister gave his daughter a shrewd look as he sipped his coffee. "You wanted to bypass us, right? In case we were so wrapped up in our problems we wouldn't take you seriously."

Frances squirmed on her chair. Sometimes her dad could see right through her.

"Well, you were right, Frances. I probably would

have laughed off the whole thing. Discouraged you when I should have been cheering you on."

Frances happily dived into the cereal her mother had set in front of her. "Tell me everything," she said. "What happened after Miss Leticia told everyone about the carnival?"

"Several other people got up and said they liked the plan too. Pops Butterfield, for one, and everybody always puts a lot of store by what he says. Mrs. Brock said the library would get behind it, and your principal said the school community would get involved."

"Did anyone speak against it?" Mrs. McAllister asked.

"Oh, a few people said it would be a waste of time, but most everyone thought it would be fun. No one knows exactly how much business it will bring in, of course, but a winter carnival is an experiment everyone seems willing to try."

"What's the next step?" Frances asked.

"The Chamber of Commerce has formed several committees. They're going to pick a date, get the publicity started, and start organizing the events."

For a moment Frances felt a little left out. After all, this whole thing had been *her* idea. But then she decided she was being silly. She knew very well she couldn't plan a winter carnival. Let the grownups handle it. They'd probably do fine.

"Do you think this will help the hardware store?" Frances asked as she swallowed a bit of cereal. It would be fun to have the carnival, of course, but helping her dad was still Frances's main objective.

Mr. McAllister smiled at her. "Well, let's put it like this. If there's going to be floats, booths, and bleachers, I guess people will be needing nails and hammers and the like."

"Oh, goody!"

It was rare enough that Frances got her parents all to herself, but the fuss they continued to make was icing on the cake. By the time Mike, Elizabeth, and Polly straggled into the kitchen, Frances felt as if she had just been named queen for a day.

"Polly, your mother should be here any minute," Mrs. McAllister said, looking at the clock. "She's going to run you home so you can change."

Polly slipped on her jacket. "I'll wait outside so she doesn't have to honk."

"Sure?" Mrs. McAllister asked. "It's very cold."

"Yes. Thanks for everything."

Frances knew Polly was anxious to get to her mother as soon as possible. She crossed her fingers and held them up as Polly turned to say good-bye to her.

As soon as Polly was out the door, Frances turned to her brother and sister. "There's going to be a winter carnival!"

Frances wasn't quite sure how the news spread around the school, but by the time she arrived there the winter carnival was already being discussed.

It was weird to hear people—kids and teachers—talking about all the upcoming fun with only the ones in her class knowing that the whole thing had originated with her. In a way, she wanted everyone to know it, but she also liked feeling anonymous. She hadn't counted on the principal, however.

Mrs. Rotterdam was so eager to fill in the details of the plans so far that she made an announcement over the intercom.

"We will be participating on many levels," she said, "staffing booths, providing entertainment, and of course partaking in all the fun activities that are being organized. This is community service at its most basic. I think you should all know that one of our very own students is responsible for this project. She discussed the idea with her ballet teacher, Miss Leticia, whom many of you know, and Miss Leticia brought it to the Chamber of Commerce. Fourth grader Frances McAllister, you can be very proud of yourself."

The whole time Mrs. Rotterdam was talking, kids kept turning around to look at her. When the principal finally clicked off, the class cheered.

Frances was embarrassed. Only an hour ago she'd been fantasizing about just this kind of attention. But now, looking around at the kids applauding her, what Frances felt most was shy. This was the kind of thing that happened to other people, not to her.

The rest of the day was strange, too. The kids who knew Frances pointed her out to the ones that didn't. Frances felt like she should be wearing a sign that said: I'M FRANCES.

When lunchtime rolled around, Frances was glad that she could get her mind off her newfound celebrity. She hadn't had a chance to talk to Polly before school started, but she had had plenty of time to observe. Though Polly had been happy about Frances's success, she had looked upset all morning. Now Frances wanted to hear all the details about Polly's talk with her mother and see if she could help.

Lena was absent today, so they had the table all to themselves. As soon as she and Polly were settled, Frances said, "So tell me. What happened?"

"She *is* seeing Mr. Winnow," Polly said flatly.

"Really!"

"Yep. She admitted it. She didn't know how to tell me because of Mr. Winnow being my teacher and all."

"Are they . . ." Frances didn't quite know how to put it. "Are they serious about each other?"

"My mother said they were just friends."

"Oh." Frances was a little disappointed. She thought it was kind of neat that Mr. Winnow and Mrs. Brock were dating.

"She's older than him, you know."

"Not by much."

"No, but still. It's gross."

"Have they gone out a lot?"

Polly played with her straw. "I didn't know how to ask that."

Frances felt bad that Polly was so unhappy. "Does Mr. Winnow know you know?"

"Yeah. He and my mother decided to tell me after we left the library yesterday." Polly made a face.

"Do you think he's going to treat you any differently?"

"I don't know."

They found out later that afternoon. Polly hadn't finished her English composition, and when she told

Mr. Winnow it wasn't done, he informed her that she was going to have to stay after school to finish it. Polly looked in Frances's direction and turned her thumb down. So much for special privileges.

Frances had her own problems that afternoon. It seemed as if ever since she found out she needed to wear glasses, her eyesight had gotten worse. Maybe that wasn't true. Maybe she just noticed her vision problems more. But one thing was certain. When their music teacher put the words to a song they were supposed to learn on the board, Frances could scarcely make out a thing.

She had started carrying her glasses around in her backpack. That was because her mother had noticed them in her drawer when she was putting away laundry. Mrs. McAllister had gotten angry and told Frances to bring them to school. With all those lines of lyrics waiting to be copied, Frances knew she had to put her glasses on. She had gotten so much good attention today, maybe no one would say anything. At least that's what Frances hoped.

She had forgotten about Albert Bell. As soon as she put her glasses on, Albert noticed.

"Hey, Specs," Albert called out. Several kids turned around and looked at him.

"Not me. Frances." Then everyone turned and looked at her.

Ducking her head, Frances pretended to be writing the words of the song in her notebook.

Miss Ford, the music teacher, rapped on the desk for attention. "Class, you're supposed to be copying down lyrics, not looking at Frances."

Frances groaned to herself. She'd gotten more than enough attention for one day. As soon as she was done with the assignment, she hastily put her glasses in her backpack. That was it, she vowed. She had worn those silly glasses for the last time.

As the class got ready to go home, Frances stopped by Polly's desk. "I'll call you later," she said.

"Okay. Are you feeling better about your glasses? Nobody really noticed them."

Frances gave her an unbelieving look.

"All right, so they noticed. But it was no big deal."

Apparently Albert didn't agree. While lining up to go outside, he managed to squeeze himself right behind her. "Four-Eyes," he sang under his breath. "Frances Four-Eyes."

"Oh, be quiet," Frances muttered. She couldn't wait to get home. It had been a long day about ten different ways.

When Frances finally got settled in the kitchen with a mug of steaming hot chocolate, she called Lena and told her everything that had gone on. It was always good to talk to Lena.

"It doesn't matter about Albert teasing you," she told Frances. "Just remember how proud everyone was of you today."

When Elizabeth arrived about half an hour later, though, *she* didn't seem very proud. "I heard Mrs. Rotterdam over the intercom," she said sourly.

Well, of course you did, Frances thought. You and everyone else in school.

"I hope you're not going to keep going on and on about it."

Frances looked at Elizabeth in amazement. She was really jealous!

"Nope, not me." But Frances couldn't resist one more dig at her sister. "Hey, did you hear that Mr. Winnow and Mrs. Brock are seeing each other?"

Elizabeth's face fell. She didn't know that Frances knew about her crush on Mr. Winnow. "Really?"

"Yep, really." Then Frances went upstairs to do her homework.

During the next few days, Frances heard a lot more about the winter carnival. Everyone seemed to have some bit of information to add. Valentine's Day fell on a Saturday, so that weekend had been reserved for the carnival. There were articles in the newspaper, and her father told her that the Chamber of Commerce was going to be doing plenty of advertising in all the surrounding counties.

Mike came home with news that the high school was going to elect a queen of the winter carnival.

"How are they going to choose her?" Elizabeth wanted to know.

"Vote. Each class is going to put up two candidates. The one with the most votes will be queen, and the two runners-up will be her court."

"Is Bambi going to run?" Frances asked.

"What do you know about Bambi?" Mike asked with a scowl.

"She *is* your girlfriend, isn't she?"

"Maybe," Mike replied curtly. That's all he would say.

There wasn't much point in having a queen without a dance, so one was scheduled at the Moose Lodge

for Saturday night. Elizabeth and Frances both cla-
mored to go.

"Aren't you a little young for that?" Mrs. Mc-
Allister said.

"No," Elizabeth and Frances said in unison.

Their mother laughed. "Well, I suppose this winter
carnival is the biggest thing to hit Lake Lister in a
long time. And of course, it *was* Frances's idea."

Frances could feel Elizabeth starting to boil.

"You can go," Mrs. McAllister continued.

Frances knew that Elizabeth would be much hap-
pier with their mother's permission if it had nothing
at all to do with Frances's bright idea. Still, you
couldn't argue with success, so Elizabeth just shrugged
and said, "Thanks, Mom."

Another development came from Miss Leticia. The
next time Frances had ballet, Miss Leticia told the
class that the recital would be held on Sunday. It
wouldn't be in the dance studio, as originally planned,
but in the Lake Lister Elementary School auditorium.

"I think we're going to need the extra space," she
said happily.

Frances had mixed emotions about this news. She
was glad that the recital was going to be a big deal,
but when she thought of all those people sitting in
the auditorium, she could feel her stomach tightening
up.

Albert, on the other hand, seemed thrilled. "Are
we going to have programs?" he asked. "Will our
pictures be in them?"

"There will be programs," Miss Leticia said. "No
pictures."

"Oh. I could draw something on the programs. You know, liven it up a little," Albert offered.

Sharks in tutus, Frances thought.

"We'll see," his aunt said.

They spent the rest of the lesson rehearsing, and Frances was amazed to observe that the promise of a big audience definitely improved Albert's performance. They went through the whole dance without Albert making one mistake—or pulling one practical joke, for that matter.

It was Frances who had problems. Without her glasses it was a little difficult to see where she was going. Twice she stumbled a bit, though she quickly corrected her mistakes.

"Hey, don't step on my toe," Albert hissed.

"I didn't."

"Not yet."

As Frances changed after practice, she knew she had a problem. It was getting too hard to see what she was doing without her glasses. The last thing she wanted to do was make a mistake during the recital, but she didn't want to get up on that stage looking like a nerd, either. Why did this have to be so complicated? she wondered. Albert, glasses, her own nervousness—there were so many things standing in the way of a good performance. Why couldn't she just get up on stage and dance?

9

rances rolled over and pulled the covers up around her neck. Maybe if she closed her eyes very tight, she could pretend she was asleep. Then she heard the small, soft whisper again.

"Oh, Frances."

Frances turned, opened one eye, and said with a sigh, "What is it, Elizabeth?"

"I thought you'd never wake up," Elizabeth said in her normal tone of voice. "Usually you're bounding out of bed."

"So today I wanted to sleep late." She looked significantly at the clock, which said eight. "It *is* Saturday. You remember Saturday—the day we don't have to go to school."

Elizabeth rolled her eyes. "I know. But I've got to talk to you."

Frances sat up in bed. There was no point in trying to sleep when Elizabeth was so keen to have a conversation. "So talk."

"I have an idea for our carnival."

"When did it get to be *our* carnival?"

"Well, it is, kind of. Isn't it? I mean the idea came from this family, and I'm certainly—"

"Elizabeth," Frances broke in, "it's the Chamber of Commerce's carnival now. They're the ones doing all the planning."

Elizabeth frowned. Frances noticed that even with a scowl on her face, her sister was awfully pretty. Some things just weren't fair.

"But this idea I have is great."

"So what is it, already?"

"I think the winter carnival queen should have a princess in her court."

"She's going to have two attendants. You know that."

"I meant a young princess." Elizabeth lowered her eyes modestly.

"No, you mean you."

"Well, maybe." Elizabeth was a little flustered.

Frances got out of bed. "I'm going to brush my teeth."

"Come on, Frannie. Hear me out."

Elizabeth rarely called Frances Frannie anymore. She must really want my help, Frances thought.

It was cold in the bedroom. Frances grabbed her flannel robe from the foot of her bed and threw it on. "How are you going to put this great idea into effect?"

"I haven't quite figured that out yet," Elizabeth said dejectedly.

"Even if you could convince Mrs. Rotterdam that we should have a princess from the elementary school, it might not be you."

Elizabeth shook her head. "If we had a princess, I'd make sure it was me."

"Well, good luck," Frances said. Her sister was probably right. She would be the princess.

"What are you doing up so early?" asked a surprised Mrs. McAllister when Frances came downstairs.

"Elizabeth woke me. And now she's gone back to sleep," Frances replied. "Are you going to work this morning?"

"I'll be at the real-estate office until twelve. Then I'm going to work at the linen store in the afternoon."

Frances sat down at the table. "I thought Daddy said last night that business was better at the store."

"It is. A little."

"Do you have to keep working two jobs?"

Mrs. McAllister took a seat across from Frances. "Oh, honey. Yes. Just because business is improving doesn't mean I should quit my jobs. If the hardware store stays busy, maybe we could use my extra money for a family vacation."

Frances thought about that for a moment. A vacation would be nice. Except for a driving trip to Minnesota two summers ago, the McAllisters hadn't been on a vacation for a long time. It would be fun to go away, especially if they went to Disney World. But as nice as that would be, having her mom home more would be better.

"I think I'd rather have you with us."

Mrs. McAllister stroked Frances's hand. "What a nice thing to say. Thank you, Frances."

"Oh, Mom," Frances said, a little embarrassed. But secretly she was pleased.

"What are you going to be doing today?"

"Polly, Lena, and I are going to make some cookies for the bake sale." On the Saturday of the carnival there were to be a number of different booths in the high school gym. Most of the activities would be taking place out on the lake, of course, but in case of really bad weather, people could go into the gym and throw darts at balloons or toss rings at milk bottles for prizes. The fourth grade was having a bake sale at their booth. Not too exciting, but it would raise money, and all the money raised at the carnival was going to charity. Lena's mother was an expert baker, and she was going to show them how to make her special sugar cookies, which the girls could freeze until the carnival next week.

Polly was already at Lena's putting on an apron when Frances arrived. Lena's house was nice, but it looked different from her house or Polly's. For one thing, there seemed to be a lot more furniture, with lace doilies on the arms of chairs and the backs of sofas. And there was only one small television in the whole house. If the McAllisters had only one television, there would be plenty of fighting. Frances was sure of it.

There were also lots of unusual pictures on the walls. Some were of religious figures, but many were photographs of the Krolls' homeland. There were so many of those pictures that Frances figured the Krolls must miss it very much.

Mrs. Kroll also seemed different from the other mothers. She always wore a dress, never pants, and she didn't smile much. Frances was a little afraid of her.

Frances wasn't late, but Mrs. Kroll was already in the kitchen looking impatient. "Ah, good, Frances, you are here. I have an apron for you, too."

"Can we make some cookies for ourselves, Mama?" Lena asked.

Now Mrs. Kroll smiled a bit. "Certainly. It wouldn't be much fun to make cookies and not get to eat any."

At first the girls were quiet, concentrating on the directions Mrs. Kroll gave them for creaming the butter with the sugar and adding the flour. But when it came time to use the cookie cutters, they started to tell Mrs. Kroll all the details of the carnival.

"Everyone's really excited about the parade," Polly said happily.

"Won't it be too cold for a parade?" Mrs. Kroll asked.

Polly shrugged. "Not if we all bundle up."

"The parade is going to be the first thing that happens."

"The booths at the high school gym will be open all day, too," Lena reminded her.

"Right. Then after the parade there will be all the contests on the lake. I'm going to enter the snowball-throwing competition," Polly said proudly.

"The dance is that night," Frances added. "And

the next day is the recital and more contests out on the lake. Lena, Polly, and I are going to try and win for best snowman."

"It sounds very nice," Mrs. Kroll said as she rolled out more dough with a big wooden rolling pin. "We used to have something like that in the town I came from."

"You did?" Lena asked with surprise.

"It wasn't in the winter. Ours was a harvest festival, but there was lots of dancing and plenty of wonderful food. And Basia."

"What's a basha?" Polly asked, wiping a speck of flour from her nose.

"Not a what," Mrs. Kroll corrected. "A who. He was a clown. He would pass out favors and make all the children laugh."

"We should have a Basia," Polly said thoughtfully.

And Frances knew who Polly thought that Basia should be. She could tell from the look on her friend's face that Polly was already picturing herself all made up in a clown costume. Elizabeth wanted to be a princess, Polly a clown. It seemed as if everybody wanted to get into the act.

That night Polly came for a sleepover at Frances's house. Mrs. Brock and Mr. Winnow, who were going out, dropped her off. Usually Elizabeth didn't pay too much attention to Frances and her friends, but as soon as Polly walked in the door, Elizabeth said, "So what's it like?"

"What?" Polly said, hanging up her coat.

"Having your mom date Mr. Winnow."

Polly didn't like to talk about it. She didn't want

any of the kids at school to find out, but she couldn't just ignore Elizabeth's direct question. "Weird," she finally said.

"Do they kiss?"

Polly made a face. "Oh, gross! I don't know."

Elizabeth got a dreamy look on her face, as if she were imagining what it might be like to kiss Mr. Winnow. Then she asked, "Where do they go on dates?"

"To the movies tonight," Polly answered shortly. Before Elizabeth could ask her anything else, Polly handed Frances a piece of colored construction paper folded in two.

"What's this?"

Polly shrugged. "It was in front of your door with a rock on it to keep it from blowing away."

Frances opened it up. SEE YOU AT THE DANCE, it read. There was a nicely drawn heart below the words. "Is this a joke, Polly?" Frances asked.

"No," Polly replied, reading it over Frances's shoulder.

Elizabeth came over to look at it. "Well, it's obviously not for you, Frances." She took the paper out of her sister's hand and smiled. "It must be for me."

Frances and Polly exchanged disgusted glances. "What makes you think that?" Frances demanded.

"Well, who in the world would send this to *you?*"

Elizabeth had a point. Frances didn't think she had any secret admirers, but she wasn't about to concede that to Elizabeth. "Maybe it's for Mike."

"Bambi could have sent it," Polly chimed in.

"I suppose," Elizabeth said huffily. She took the paper anyway. "But I still think it's for me."

Polly watched her waltz upstairs. "At least she doesn't think Mr. Winnow sent it."

Frances and Polly walked into the den. "I know it's hard for you, Polly. I mean, seeing your mom dating Mr. Winnow."

"It's just kind of embarrassing. For both of us, I think."

"He doesn't treat you special in class."

"He sure doesn't. He told me in the car coming over here that he knows this is awkward, but he thinks I'm handling it really well."

"Mr. Winnow is awfully nice."

"I know." Polly sighed. "But I still liked him better when he was just my teacher."

Frances turned on the television. It was hard to see the TV from where she was sitting, so she pulled her glasses down from the top of her head, where she had been wearing them lately.

Mrs. McAllister had mentioned Frances's lack of glasses at home about a week ago.

"Frances, I know I've been working a lot lately, but I'm around enough to notice I rarely see you with your glasses on," she had said.

"Oh, I wear them," Frances said vaguely.

Her mother had folded her arms and given Frances her sternest look. "I want to see you wearing them. Now."

So Frances had taken to wearing them on the top

of her head, the way movie stars wore their sunglasses. She usually remembered to push them down when her mom was around.

Mr. Winnow had wondered about them too, so now at school she kept them on her desk in their case. When she had to, in order to see something important, she put them on. But only when she absolutely had to. And she wanted to see this movie, so on they went.

Polly looked at her critically. "You know, they really don't look that bad on you."

"They don't look that good, either."

"Have you decided if you're going to wear them in the recital?" Frances had shared all her worries on that topic with her friend.

"I don't know."

"You're going to be the best dancer in that whole recital, glasses or not," Polly said loyally.

Frances smiled. "Thanks." Then her smile faded. "Too bad I'm going to have the worst dancer right next to me."

The last few days before the winter carnival were a flurry of activity at home and at school—all through Lake Lister, actually.

All over downtown banners were going up welcoming the expected visitors.

"People *are* going to come, aren't they?" Frances asked anxiously one night at dinner.

"I hope so," Mr. McAllister replied. "The dance on Saturday night is sold out, so that's a good sign."

"I saw Miss Leticia on the street," Mrs. McAllister

added. "She's only got a few tickets left for the recital."

Frances could feel herself getting a little tense over that news, but Elizabeth said, "Great! And my campaign to be a princess at the carnival is moving right along too."

Frances couldn't believe her sister's boldness. Earlier that week, Elizabeth had asked Mrs. Rotterdam if she could be a princess, and the principal had said no. "What if everyone wanted to be a princess?" she had asked.

Elizabeth was discouraged at first, but then she had another idea. At breakfast the next day she had handed Frances a piece of paper. "Sign this, will you?"

"What is it?" Frances asked, glancing at a page Elizabeth had decorated with colored-pencil flowers.

"My petition."

"Your . . ." Frances read aloud the several sentences Elizabeth had written. "We, the undersigned, feel that Lake Lister Elementary School should have a representative in the queen's court at the winter carnival dance." Frances looked up. "You think this will work?"

"Sure," Elizabeth said confidently. "You know how big Mrs. Rotterdam is on democracy. Well, this is democracy in action."

"But this doesn't say anything about you being the princess," Frances pointed out.

"Well, no. But after I've done all the work, Mrs. Rotterdam can't help but pick me."

There was no arguing with Elizabeth when she was in a mood like this. Frances just signed the petition.

Polly, too, was going ahead with her plans to be a clown at the carnival, but she wasn't even going to try to go through channels. "I found one of my old Halloween costumes," she told Frances excitedly on Thursday morning. "It'll be great."

"But what are you going to do at the carnival?" Frances asked as they walked to school.

"I'm not sure yet. Something good, though," she said, and smiled.

Frances was a little worried about Polly getting in trouble with this Basia business, but she decided that worrying was a waste of time. Polly usually landed on her feet whatever was happening.

The first bell was ringing as Frances went to her desk. Sitting on top of it was a piece of colored construction paper folded in half. Just like the one that came to the house, Frances thought, confused. She opened it up. TWO MORE DAYS UNTIL THE DANCE, it read.

Frances jerked her head up and took a quick look around the room. No one seemed to be looking in her direction or paying any attention to her at all. Her eyes fell suspiciously on Polly. After all, Polly was known for her practical jokes, and she was the only one who knew about the first note.

But Polly was frantically trying to finish her math homework. Besides, the two of them had walked in together. There would have been no chance for Polly to put the note on her desk.

Frances looked at it once more, then shoved the piece of paper inside her desk. Who in the world could have sent it?

10

throughout English, math, and spelling, Frances tried to figure out the answer to that question, but none came to mind. Logic said that the note was left by someone in the class, but as Frances looked over the boys one by one, it didn't seem possible that it could have been sent by any of them. Maybe Tammi or Sheila did it as a gag.

Frances couldn't wait until she, Lena, and Polly were settled at lunch. She pulled out the piece of paper and told Lena about what had happened on Saturday night.

"You're kidding," Lena said, taking the note and reading it herself.

"Ooooh," squealed Polly. "Someone has a crush on you."

"It's probably a joke," Frances said.

"I don't think so," Lena said. "This seems very sincere to me."

The girls spent the rest of the lunch period trying

to figure out who could have sent it, but they didn't come up with one possibility.

"I guess we'll just have to wait until the dance," Polly said as she gathered her trash from lunch to throw in the garbage.

Frances decided to try and forget the whole thing. It made her too nervous to think about it. Of course, there were already several things she was trying not to think about—the recital and the success of the winter carnival. If things didn't go well, Frances was afraid people might blame her.

By the next day—Friday—Frances was having trouble keeping her mind on anything. She kept re-playing her dance steps over and over in her head, wishing as usual that it wasn't Albert Bell she saw dancing next to her.

She also worried about Polly and what she was going to do when she had her clown outfit on. Polly was still keeping her plans to herself.

Then there was Elizabeth, who was all excited about her petition. She had informed Frances at breakfast that she had more than fifty signatures and was going to present the list to Mrs. Rotterdam today.

"She still doesn't know anything about it?" Frances asked.

"Nope. It's going to be a surprise." Elizabeth winked. "That's part of my strategy, taking her by surprise."

Frances just shook her head. She hoped that it wasn't Elizabeth who turned out to be surprised.

She didn't think about the mysterious note, though, until she walked into the classroom. Was there going to be another folded piece of construction paper waiting on her desk? she wondered.

Heaving a sigh of relief, Frances saw that her desk-top was as empty as she had left it the day before. Maybe the silly joker, whoever he or she was, had decided to give up.

Knowing how excited his fourth grade was, Mr. Winnow kept the work to a minimum. They discussed their bake-sale booth. Kids had signed up for hour shifts to work the booth so that they could spend most of the day enjoying the carnival. Then Mr. Winnow read aloud from a funny book, *Tales of a Fourth Grade Nothing*. They did a little history and a few math games. Despite the easy day, time still seemed to pass slowly. Finally the last bell rang.

"All right, class, I'll see you all at the carnival tomorrow."

There was more noise than usual as the fourth grade got their coats and hurried out of the building.

One of the first people Frances saw in the hall was Elizabeth. She didn't look happy.

"What happened?" Frances asked. "Did you give Mrs. Rotterdam your petition?"

Elizabeth nodded. "I did," she said grimly.

"Tell me."

"Well, she looked over the petition and said, 'You might be right, Elizabeth. Maybe we do need a representative from the school.' "

"But she didn't pick you?"

"No!" Elizabeth burst out. "She picked Tina Soderberg."

"But she's in the first grade!"

"That's right. Mrs. Rotterdam said a *little* princess would be adorable in the queen's court."

Frances tried to hide a smile because Elizabeth looked so mad. But it was kind of funny.

"Boy, the next time Mrs. Rotterdam starts talking about democracy in action . . ." Elizabeth shook her head and walked toward her locker.

The first thing Frances did when she got up the next morning was look out the window. All week she had been hoping for good weather. That meant not bitter cold and not so warm that the snow would melt. It also meant no fresh snow, which might keep visitors away.

To her relief it was a bright, sunny day. The snow, which didn't seem to be melting at all, sparkled like diamonds. At least the weather was on her side.

Hurrying downstairs, Frances wasn't surprised to see her family gathered around the kitchen table passing pieces of the newspaper back and forth. The weekend insert listed all the carnival activities.

"I'm going to win something at the snowball throw," Mike said. "It's at two o'clock."

"You're going to win something for Bambi, you mean," Elizabeth said slyly.

"Maybe *I'll* go and win something for *my* girl," Mr. McAllister said, patting his wife's hand.

Mrs. McAllister noticed Frances. "Sleepyhead, I thought you were going to miss all the fun."

"Not me," Frances declared. "I have to be at the bake-sale booth from nine to ten. Then I want to go downtown and watch the parade. Then I'm going to the ice sculpture contest—"

"Sounds like you've got a full schedule, honey," Mr. McAllister said.

"You don't have to work all day, do you, Dad?" Frances asked anxiously.

"Your mom's going to spell me for a while, and one of the clerks will come in for part of the day. I'll be able to see plenty."

"Good."

"Don't forget the dance," Elizabeth reminded them. "Everybody's going to be there."

"Now we just have to see how many people come to everything else," Frances said nervously.

By the time she finished up at the bake-sale booth and walked downtown, Frances had her answer. The sidewalks were packed with people all bundled up and ready for the parade to begin.

Frances was supposed to meet Polly and Lena at the Sweet Shoppe, but it was so full of people buying hot chocolate and coffee to take away that Frances couldn't find them.

Then a swirl of polka-dotted fabric caught her eye. She had forgotten there was going to be an easy way to spot Polly—she was dressed as a clown.

"Hey, happy winter carnival," Polly called to Frances, waving wildly. She pulled Lena along with her to where Frances was standing.

It took Frances a moment to take in Polly's costume. Not only was she wearing a polka-dot clown suit and a matching hat, but she was all made up with a chalk-white face and a big droopy red mouth. Polly looked fat, too, but Frances realized that it was just because Polly was wearing her down jacket under the costume.

"What do you think?" she asked, whirling around.

"It's great," Frances said sincerely.

"She's being a real Basia," Lena informed Frances. "She's handing out candies to the little children and making all the grownups laugh."

It warmed Frances's heart to think about the whole town getting so involved in the winter carnival. It didn't really seem like her carnival anymore, but as Frances watched the floats come riding down Main Street, she knew it didn't matter. It was everyone's now.

After a hard day of laughing and playing, Frances was so tired that she almost wanted to forgo the dance. If she didn't go, she'd never learn who her secret admirer was, of course, but maybe that was a good thing.

In the end, though, she had to go, because her mother didn't want her to stay home alone. Nervously she got dressed. She had decided to wear her new blue skirt and a soft white sweater her grandmother had given her for Christmas. In her hair she wore a sparkly headband borrowed from Elizabeth.

The lodge was already full when the McAllisters arrived. By the time she had hung up her coat she had said hello to Pops Butterfield, Mrs. Rotterdam, and several kids in her class. Then she spotted Lena and Polly in the corner. Waving good-bye to her family, she hurried over to her friends.

"Pretty neat, huh?" Polly said as Frances walked up.

"This place looks great," Frances agreed.

The lodge had been transformed into a winter wonderland. Glittery snowflakes hung from the ceiling and large Styrofoam snowmen smiled at the action from the corners of the room. A band made up of college students was playing noisily while people danced in the middle of the floor.

"I wonder where your secret admirer is," Polly said, glancing around the room.

Frances shrugged, trying to look as if she couldn't care less. "I told you it was all a joke." But as the evening wore on, Frances couldn't help but look over her shoulder every time the band started a new number. Just when she decided all the notes really had been a joke, she felt a tap on her shoulder.

"Here I am."

Frances whirled around and faced Albert Bell.

Polly and Lena, who were standing next to her at the refreshment table having some punch and cookies, looked shocked. Frances supposed she looked the same.

"What do you mean?" she asked, finally finding her voice.

"I'm here for my dance."

"You sent those notes!"

"Yep." Albert grinned.

Frances turned away. "Very funny."

"Hey, I wasn't kidding. I want to dance with you."

Frances looked at her friends with stricken eyes. Polly found her voice first. "Why do you want to dance with her?"

"None of your business, Broccoli." He tugged at Frances's hand. "Come on."

Helplessly Frances followed Albert onto the dance floor. Fortunately the band was playing a fast number. She would have just died if it had been a slow dance. If the band wasn't playing so loudly, she might have tried to say something to Albert. Instead she just watched him shimmy and shake, dancing with much more enthusiasm than he had ever shown at ballet class. Frances, who wasn't used to this kind of dancing, just sort of swung her arms and shuffled her feet, trying to look unconcerned.

When the music stopped, Albert cheerfully said, "Well, thanks," and turned to walk away.

"Wait a minute." Frances's voice was so firm it surprised her.

"What?"

"How come you sent me those notes?"

Albert shrugged. "Cause I wanted to dance with you. And I figured if I just came up to you tonight, you probably wouldn't."

That was true, Frances thought.

"So I figured if I sent you those notes, you'd be kind of like, you know, prepared."

Frances wondered how anyone could be prepared to dance with Albert.

Polly and Lena had been waiting impatiently for Frances to rejoin them after the dance.

"What did he say?" Polly demanded.

Frances repeated what Albert said.

"I think he likes you," Lena said shyly.

"No!"

"Yes, he does," Polly insisted. "Albert Bell likes you." She hooted. "Can you believe it?"

Lying in bed later that night, Frances stared at the ceiling, unable to sleep. Albert Bell had actually been nice. Well, he hadn't been mean, at any rate. She wondered if they had ever had a conversation since kindergarten without any teasing. She couldn't remember it if they had.

Frances drifted off to sleep with Polly's words ringing in her ears. "Can you believe it?"

11

frances stared into the bathroom mirror. The recital was in less than two hours, and Frances wanted to make sure she wasn't getting the chickenpox. Or the mumps or measles.

She had gotten up so early that it seemed as if she had been lying there for hours before it started to get light. That's when she had realized she wasn't feeling well, although she wasn't quite sure if she felt feverish or if her stomach hurt. Did you get stomachache with the measles? she wondered.

Elizabeth had lain snoring away on the other side of the room. Apparently she was feeling perfectly fine.

Frances turned away from the mirror. She didn't see any spots or bumps. Besides, people were counting on her to be at the recital. Miss Leticia, even Albert, maybe.

Albert. How was she ever going to face him? Then there was the matter of her glasses. Was she going to wear them or not? Frances wanted to do nothing so much as go back to bed, pull the covers over her head, and stay there.

"Hey." Elizabeth banged on the bathroom door. "Could you hurry up in there? I have to get ready too, you know."

Frances opened the door. "It's all yours."

Elizabeth glanced at her sister curiously. "You look kind of weird."

"I do?" Frances said hopefully.

"Yes, like you're really worried about something."

"Oh."

"You don't have stage fright, do you?" she teased.

Frances pushed past her sister. "No, I don't."

Mrs. McAllister was putting the laundry away in the linen closet. "That's enough, Elizabeth." She followed Frances into the bedroom and closed the door.

"Frances, I know I haven't been around a lot lately, so I haven't had a chance to tell you how proud I am of you."

"You are?"

"Of course I am. Why shouldn't I be? You got this whole carnival project going, and you're dancing the lead in the recital. I remember when you would have been much too shy to get up on the stage in front of everyone."

Frances put her arms around her mother's waist. "I might still be too shy," she whispered.

Her mother stroked her hair. It felt good. "I don't think so. Not any more."

There was something in the way her mother said those words that made Frances believe them too. Mrs.

McAllister looked down at her daughter. "There is one thing I've been worrying about."

"What?"

"Like I said, I know I haven't been around a lot, Frances, and we've talked about this before, but you're still not wearing your glasses the way you're supposed to."

Frances pulled away. "Oh, Mom! I wear them."

"You're not wearing them now," her mother pointed out.

"I look funny in them."

"Have the kids been teasing you?"

"Not really." Frances had to tell the truth. No one besides Albert had said anything, and even he didn't pay much attention now when she wore them in class.

"Frances, it's important that you take care of your eyesight."

"But I'm supposed to wear them almost all the time. Like at the recital today. I can't do that."

"Why not?"

"Whoever heard of a dancer in glasses?"

"Whoever heard of a dancer squinting and stumbling around onstage?"

"Do you think that would happen?" Frances asked in horror.

"You do squint when you can't see, which is whenever you're not wearing your glasses."

"But I'll look stupid," Frances wailed.

"Honey, I can't go backstage with you and tape your glasses to your nose."

Even Frances had to smile at that.

"But you'd better think about whether or not it would be best to wear them. When you're older we can consider contact lenses, but right now the simple fact is that glasses help you see. I think you want to see during the recital, don't you?"

Frances knew what her mother wanted her to do, but as she continued to get ready, and on her way to the recital, a battle was raging inside her head. Would she look stupider appearing onstage in her glasses or stumbling around?

The winter carnival was continuing on Main Street, and while there wasn't as much activity as the day before, Lake Lister still had a festive air. The school auditorium was quite full too, Frances noticed as she slipped backstage.

Miss Leticia, dressed in a short black gown, was trying to keep order as students from her classes got into their costumes and makeup. "Quiet, *s'il vous plaît,*" she kept stage-whispering. "The audience is arriving."

Frances was already wearing her blue tights and felt skirt and frilly white blouse, but there were still her ballet slippers to put on. When she looked up, there stood Albert in his costume—a white shirt and a pair of shorts.

"Can you believe this?" Albert asked with disgust. "If I knew I had to wear *shorts* . . ."

"Didn't your aunt tell you?"

"Not till this morning. I thought I was just going to be wearing pants."

This was the opportunity that Frances had been waiting for. Here was the perfect chance to tease

Albert just the way he had always teased her. But he looked so woebegone that she didn't have the heart to start making fun of him. Instead she said something that surprised even her. "I might look stupid myself."

"What do you mean?"

"If I wear my glasses," Frances said, her voice low.

"Aw, wear them."

"Do you think I should?"

"They don't look that bad. Besides, I told you, I don't want you stepping all over me."

Frances smiled a little.

"Anyway, if you wear your glasses, maybe the audience won't look at my knees." He made his very visible knees wiggle up and down.

Suddenly it was all very clear to Frances. She needed to wear her glasses to see properly. It was as simple as that. Who cared if she was the first dancer to wear glasses? There had to be a first time for everything.

When the curtain rose, Albert, his knees exposed, and Frances, her glasses firmly in place, began their dance. If the audience thought either of them looked funny, they didn't show it.

It was one of those times when Frances just knew she was doing everything right. All through the dance she could feel herself responding perfectly to the music. Even Albert seemed to be dancing and not just walking through it like he usually did. After the dance ended—with no mistakes—there was loud applause.

Frances and Albert took a bow, then hurried offstage.

"Boy, I'm glad that's over." Albert was sweating.

"I'm not," Frances said, her eyes shining. "I'd like to do it again."

That evening the McAllisters sat around the kitchen table eating apple pie and rehashing the weekend events.

"I thought my dance went perfectly," Elizabeth said.

"If you do say so yourself." Mike laughed.

"Both of my girls did a good job," Mr. McAllister said firmly.

"Did you do a lot of business this weekend?" Frances asked.

"Some. The last few weeks have been good, though, what with all the activity. And lots of people who came in said they'd be back. I don't think we're out of the woods yet, but we may be on the way."

"I was telling Frances this morning how proud we are of her," Mrs. McAllister said.

"Yeah, we are," Mike said gruffly.

Frances looked around at her family and smiled. "Oh, I just had a good idea. And then it snow-balled."

ILENE COOPER has written several children's books including the acclaimed *Kids from Kennedy Middle School* series. She has also written for television and is currently the children's book editor at *Booklist* magazine. When she's not reading or writing, she's knitting or traveling in England, her favorite country. She lives in Highland Park, Illinois, with her husband, a television director.

Wanted: One best friend

Frances in the Fourth Grade

FRANCES TAKES A CHANCE

by Ilene Cooper

Frances McAllister has always been shy, but she's always had her best friend, Bonnie, there to help her out. Now that Bonnie has moved away and practically ruined her life, Frances isn't sure how she's going to survive. Just when she starts to think that this is going to be the worst year of her life, Frances meets Polly Brock. Polly's new in town, and she wants to be Frances's friend. The only problem is Polly's a little overwhelming. Could Frances's first real friend in the fourth grade be more than she can handle?

F I R S T   T I M E   I N   P R I N T !

A BULLSEYE BOOK PUBLISHED BY ALFRED A. KNOPF, INC.

Friends through thick and thin...

Frances in the Fourth Grade

FRANCES DANCES

by Ilene Cooper

Ever since Frances McAllister saw *Swan Lake,* she's dreamed of becoming a ballet dancer. So when Miss Leticia's School of the Dance opens downtown, Frances is thrilled. But there's just one problem—Frances is so shy that the thought of performing in front of a bunch of strangers makes her feel sick. Would it help if Polly took lessons with her? Frances thinks so. So what if Polly doesn't like ballet—best friends are supposed to do everything together, aren't they?

F I R S T   T I M E   I N   P R I N T !

A BULLSEYE BOOK PUBLISHED BY ALFRED A. KNOPF, INC.

Make friends with—

FRANCES IN THE FOURTH GRADE

by Ilene Cooper

Meet Frances McAllister—she's small and shy, and she's not sure she can survive fourth grade without her best friend by her side. Then she meets the outgoing Polly Brock...and somehow life won't ever be the same. Share a whole year of fun and surprises with Frances and her friends! Collect all four books!